Charity's eyes widened, and forbidden images popped into her head. Fascinatingly masculine images.

"Unfortunately, with this shackle around my ankle, I won't be able to get my pants off."

"What a pity," she said drily.

"I knew you'd be disappointed."

What she was was a nervous wreck.

By the time they got into bed, her mouth was dry and her heart was beating as if she had a severe case of old-maid palpitations. She could barely draw a steady breath.

Garrett was impossibly large in her double bed, his broad shoulders and enticingly bare chest taking up far more than his half of the space. Her mind kept cycling over the awareness that this was—or should have been—his wedding night.

And the foolish, impossible fantasy of *her* being his bride.

Dear Reader,

In the tiny Western town of Grazer's Corners, something is happening.... Weddings are in the air—and the town's most eligible bachelors are running for cover!

Three popular American Romance authors have put together a rollicking good time in THE BRIDES OF GRAZER'S CORNERS. On the satin-pump heels of Jacqueline Diamond's *The Cowboy & The Shotgun Bride* and Mindy Neff's *A Bachelor for the Bride*, this month Charlotte Maclay brings you *The Hog-Tied Groom*.

If you missed any of these titles, you can order them by sending $3.99 U.S./$4.50 CAN. to Harlequin Reader Service at 3010 Walden Av., P.O. Box 1325, Buffalo, NY 14269 or P.O. Box 609, Fort Erie, Ont. L2A 5X3 Canada.

You're invited to all three weddings.... Who'll catch the bouquet next?

Happy reading!

Debra Matteucci
Senior Editor & Editorial Coordinator
Harlequin Books
300 East 42nd Street
New York, NY 10017

The Hog-Tied Groom

CHARLOTTE MACLAY

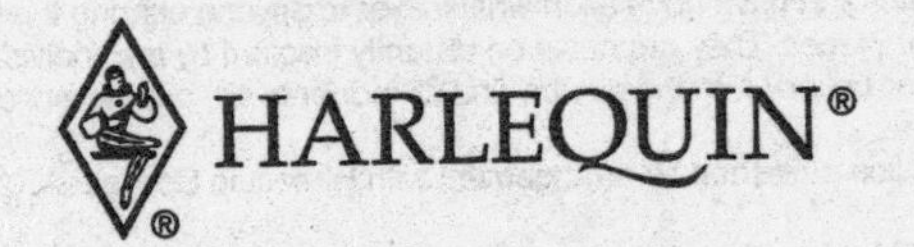

TORONTO • NEW YORK • LONDON
AMSTERDAM • PARIS • SYDNEY • HAMBURG
STOCKHOLM • ATHENS • TOKYO • MILAN • MADRID
PRAGUE • WARSAW • BUDAPEST • AUCKLAND

ISBN 0-373-16743-1

THE HOG-TIED GROOM

This edition published by arrangement with Harlequin Books S.A.

Printed in U.S.A.

Chapter One

If she hadn't needed the money so much, Charity Arden would never have agreed to photograph Garrett Keeley's wedding that afternoon.

She remembered all too well how the camera loved his ruggedly handsome good looks. The devil-may-care twinkle in his eyes and that cocky grin slipped right past the welcoming lens, imprinting themselves on the film in the same way they left their mark on a woman's heart.

She ought to know, she thought as she checked to be sure she had enough film to properly record Garrett's wedding to Hailey Olson. Of course, if things went as they had these past two weeks in Grazer's Corners, yet another bride would vanish from the church, dragged off to who knew where by people unknown, and Charity would be out another job as official wedding photographer, losing the income that went with it.

"At this rate, I could be flat broke in a month," she mumbled, twisting the focus rings on her camera to make sure they were all functioning perfectly.

The morning sun drifted through the lace curtains of the old farmhouse that was her home. Her studio and darkroom were nearby in the barn. Dust motes danced in the air like a summer blizzard.

These wedding-day disasters were costing Charity a fortune in film that wasn't worth developing, though the *Grazer Gazette* had purchased one shot of debutante Jordan Grazer in full wedding regalia leaping onto a motorcycle behind a leather-jacketed hunk—name unknown.

That picture had made a perfect companion piece on the front page of the weekly newspaper for Charity's slightly out-of-focus photo of the presumed gangster who had made off the previous week with the newly elected town sheriff, Kate Bingham.

But none of that had produced anything like the income two full sets of wedding photos would have generated.

On the good-news side, the only person she could imagine kidnapping Hailey Olson would be Charity's brother, Bud. He'd have more sense. She hoped. Forget that Bud and Hailey had been an item some years ago. Parental disapproval on Hailey's side had quashed any future for that romance.

After all, crossing the metaphorical tracks in Grazer's Corners was a real stretch. Bud and Charity, and their pig farm, definitely sat on the *wrong* side.

Checking her watch, she wondered where said brother was. She was counting on Bud to return home by the time she had to leave.

She picked up her khaki fisherman's vest from the old oak dining table and checked the pockets to make sure her assorted filters were in place. She'd be taking some of the photos outdoors on the town square across from the church and she wanted to be sure—

At the sound of a vehicle on the gravel driveway, she glanced outside. Bud's battered panel truck was just coming to a stop at the front of the house.

Relieved he'd made it home in time, she went back to checking her equipment. A few moments later, she became aware of particularly heavy footsteps on the porch. The steps creaked more loudly than usual. The planks groaned. Finally the screen door squeaked open.

Looking up, she stared at her brother. "Why on earth are you bringing a sack of feed in here? Take that on out back and—"

Her mouth clamped shut.

Two legs stuck out of the feed sack Bud had slung over his shoulder—legs tied together with a thick rope and dressed in tuxedo pants with a black stripe down the side. The sack's occupant was wearing shiny black leather shoes—shoes big enough to belong to a man fully as tall and big as Bud, who measured six foot-plus and weighed well over two hundred pounds. All of it solid muscle.

Charity did not like the feel of this.

"What have you done, Bud?"

The feed sack uttered an unintelligible sound.

"You've gotta help me, sis."

She shook her head. "I don't think so." Fraternal love had its limits, including serving a lifetime sentence for kidnapping. And she had a horrible, sinking feeling that was exactly what was taking place in front of her astonished eyes.

None too gently, Bud lowered his burden to the living-room couch. It wasn't a particularly comfortable couch. The cushions were lumpy, with one or two springs threatening breakout.

The sack groaned.

"You can't do this, Bud."

"Hailey and I have it all figured out." Her brother straightened and flexed his shoulders—the broad shoulders of a man who worked a subsistence farm before and after an eight-hour shift on the job that really paid the bills. "She's leaving a note for her folks saying she and Garrett are impatient and didn't want to mess with all the formal wedding stuff. So they're eloping."

They? Charity suspected it was Bud and Hailey who were on the lam.

Gazing at the feed sack, noting long legs and the outline of shoulders almost as broad as Bud's, Charity knew her first guess had been right. "That's Garrett in there, isn't it?"

The sack grunted affirmatively.

"You've got to keep him here, sis. Two or three days."

Days? She nearly choked on the idea. "I can't do that!"

"Sure, you can. All we need is a chance to get married in Las Vegas and then..." A crimson flush stole up her brother's suntanned cheeks. "You know, consummate the marriage. After that, her folks can't do anything—"

"How 'bout getting a judge to send you to prison for the rest of your life for kidnapping?"

More affirmative grunts from the captive in the sack. Loud ones. With his feet hog-tied together, Garrett banged his heels on the living-room floor hard enough to shake the whole house.

"I'm not kidnapping Hailey. She wants to marry me."

"You've *kidnapped* Garrett, Bud," she wailed. "You could go to jail—"

"There's no sheriff in town. Once this has all settled down, I'll work it out with Garrett—" the sack shook its entire torso negatively "—and with Hailey's folks. It'll be all right. You'll see."

Charity didn't think so.

Hoping to avoid getting kicked, she approached the kidnap victim cautiously. Apparently his arms were tied behind his back, or he would have been doing even more flailing. She tugged at the feed sack until she could pull it free.

Garrett had unfairly attractive eyes with long, sandy-brown lashes and squint lines at the corners. Normally Charity thought of his eyes as hazel with a few flecks of gold, though sometimes they could look almost green. Now, through some trick of the light, they appeared black.

And furious.

He grunted a string of sounds that were no doubt unpleasantly descriptive expletives. A wide piece of silver duct tape across his mouth prevented him from expressing himself more clearly. Not that she had any trouble understanding his thoughts.

He was going to kill Bud the first chance he got. Then he'd probably strangle Charity, too.

She sighed. If the truth were known, she'd been no more happy about the marriage of Garrett and Hailey than her brother had. But for far different reasons and without any right to feel that way.

"We can't do this, Bud."

Garrett shot daggers at Bud, then included Charity

in the barrage. That hurt. Couldn't he tell she was trying to talk her brother out of his crazy scheme?

"Sorry, sis. For a lot of stuff." He darted a glance at Garrett, then back to his sister. "But Hailey and I love each other. This is how it's got to be."

Bud produced a set of leg irons like those worn by chain gangs. He shoved the coffee table out of the way and knelt in front of Garrett.

"Where'd you get those?" Charity asked.

Garrett's eyes widened; he kicked at Bud with his feet.

"From the sheriff's office. Nobody's there these days. Door's unlocked."

"No, Bud," Charity warned. She grabbed her brother's shoulder and tried to push him away. His well-muscled frame wouldn't budge. "You're carrying this whole thing too far."

One heavy metal bracelet snapped closed around Garrett's right ankle. The two-foot-long chain rattled.

"For heaven's sake, Bud, you can't—"

The second cuff snapped into place around Charity's left ankle.

"No! Are you crazy—?"

"I love you, sis. Three days." Standing, Bud brushed a quick kiss to her cheek, then backed toward the front door. "That's all I need. And maybe...well, maybe other things will work out, too."

"What are you talking about? You can't do this. Give me the key, Bud. You've taken this joke far enough." Good heavens! She didn't want to be shackled to Garrett Keeley for three days. Not even for three minutes!

A series of grunts emphasized Garrett's full agreement.

"Sorry, sis. There's lots of feed in the shed for the pigs. You won't be needing to go to town, so I disabled your car. The phone, too." With a sheepish shrug, he turned and went out the door.

"Bud!"

She ran after him. And made it all of two feet before she went splat on the floor, her ankle still firmly chained to Garrett's. The air left her lungs.

Somehow Garrett managed to get to his feet. Grunting what sounded like a whole string of orders, he hopped in the direction Bud had fled. But Charity hadn't regained her breath yet and was still flat on the floor. When Garrett reached the limits of the chain, he went down to his knees.

Twisting, he glared at her. Obviously he was no more pleased with the situation than she was. Understandably. But Lord help her, Bud had never asked another thing of her in his entire life. Her big brother had been her protector, her friend, someone she could rely on when times got tough. He'd been there for her ever since their mother had deserted them and, as orphans, they'd moved to the farm to live with their grandparents.

Now Bud had asked a favor of Charity without knowing all the implications of his request. Because she had never *told* him.

Too late to say no, she thought grimly.

"Why don't I take off the duct tape?" she suggested as a beginning step to calm Garrett's fury.

He nodded.

"But no yelling at me. This wasn't my idea. I'm a victim here, too."

His grunt sounded somewhat calmer.

Her fingers trembled slightly as she caught the edge of the tape. She hadn't been this close to Garrett for more than eight years. His eyes were on her, studying her, still blazing with fury. He wore his hair a little longer than he used to, expertly styled to allow the variegated blond waves to curl at his nape. Waves like warm velvet, she recalled.

She gave the tape a hard tug and dragged it off all at once.

"Ouch! Dammit!" Lifting his shoulder, he wiped one side of his mouth on his tuxedo shirt. Diamond studs marched down the stiff front. "You didn't have to take all the skin off, too."

"Look on the bright side," she quipped. "I've just waxed your mustache for you. Women pay good money for—"

"You know I'm going to kill your brother when I get my hands on him," he interrupted.

She grimaced. "I figured you'd feel that way."

"Yeah." Garrett glanced around the room, fury and frustration seething in his gut as he sat there on the floor feeling like a fool. The truck had already driven away, Bud behind the wheel—presumably Garrett's bride-to-be waiting for him somewhere down the road. This was the damnedest mess Garrett had ever gotten himself in. Hell on his ego to have his bride run off with some other guy two hours before the wedding. "I thought it was the women in this town who got kidnapped on their wedding day."

"Guess you're the exception that makes the rule."

Smart mouth!

From two feet away, she met his gaze levelly with her toffee brown eyes. Her lips didn't so much as twitch at the "joke" her brother had played on Garrett. And on her, too, he realized.

"You didn't know what Bud was up to?" he asked.

"Not a clue. I was just getting my gear ready for the wedding." She nodded toward the dining-room table and her camera.

It looked like she was telling the truth. But how could Bud and Hailey have pulled off this body-snatching job without *somebody* knowing it was coming? "Think you can get me untied?"

"Sure."

He turned his back so she could work on the rope Bud had bound around his wrists. He'd never been in Charity's house before. It was an old farmhouse east of Grazer's Corners, close enough to the Sierra foothills to be able to see them on days when the San Joaquin Valley wasn't too hazy. And far enough from town to keep the smell of pigs away from the folks who lived there. Most of the time.

The house was like the farm, a little run-down. The hodgepodge of furniture might have been new in the 1930s but now looked worn. Except for an overflowing stack of *Farm Journal* magazines, the place was neat enough and there was a hint of cinnamon in the air. Or maybe that was Charity's scent he was catching, kind of spicy and fresh.

He wished she'd get the damn knot loose. He hadn't seen Charity in a long time, but he remembered....

"Can you hurry it up a bit? I'd like to get untied before the next rains come." Given the dry summers in central California, that would be months from now.

"It would be easier with a knife. You don't happen to have one on you, do you?"

"In my pocket."

There was a very long pause, the silence dragging out for several heartbeats. Garrett knew she was considering sliding her hand in his pants pocket. If he hadn't been so damn mad about being kidnapped by her brother, he might have enjoyed the thought. But not now.

"Why don't we try to make it into the kitchen?" she suggested, breaking the silence. "I've got a sharp butcher knife that should do the trick."

"Okay. You get up first."

She did that easily enough. He was going to have much more trouble, trying to maneuver himself to his feet, particularly with his bum knee. He'd already landed on it once. The recently repaired joint couldn't take much more pounding.

Using all the muscles and flexibility he'd honed during his abbreviated NFL football career, he heaved himself to his feet. He wobbled, fighting for balance. Charity steadied him. She stood about five-seven, and he could feel she had a lot of strength in her arms. She wasn't anything like Hailey, who was on the petite side and wore designer clothes, carefully manicured nails and artfully applied makeup.

Charity had always seemed more elementally female, an earth-mother type. A single braid hung down her back, loosely tied, her hair golden brown like weak coffee when the sun caught it just right. Her sundress was plain at best, though it did show off her tanned shoulders nicely. Overall, Charity was not Garrett's usual style.

"You ready to try?" she asked.

"Why not?"

He hopped. She steadied him. He hopped again.

"You know, under different circumstances, this would be pretty funny," she said.

He hopped. "I'm not amused." The chain dragged across the worn hardwood floor.

"Neither am I. But it *is* a little like a kids' three-legged race. I used to start laughing so hard in those, I'd always fall down and couldn't finish the race."

"Ha-ha." Hell, he'd lost his career only months ago and now he'd lost the woman he was going to marry. If his sense of humor was a little off, he'd damn well earned the right. He'd told Hailey he *loved* her. Hadn't that been enough?

They'd reached the kitchen, and Charity opened a drawer near the sink, pulling out a knife.

"I hope you're not contemplating any kind of revenge," he muttered.

Tilting her head, she gave him an unreadable look. "The thought of revenge has never crossed my mind," she said with complete seriousness.

She reached behind him, and a moment later his hands came free. Tossing aside the remnants of rope, Garrett rubbed his wrists until the burning sensation of returning circulation eased.

"Geez, that's better. Give me the knife." She stood quietly beside him while he cut through the rope at his ankles. "Okay, now we need a hacksaw so we can get these ankle bracelets off."

"I don't have one."

He eyed her suspiciously. "Okay. A sledgehammer and chisel will do. Or bolt cutters."

"Sorry."

"What? You live on a farm and you don't have a hacksaw? Or bolt cutters? What gives?"

"Bud wanted me to keep you here for three days."

"You're joking, right?"

She shook her head. "I wish I were."

"I'm going to get rid of this chain-gang routine and then I'm going after Hailey. If I have to go into town to find somebody to unlock these damn cuffs or cut 'em off, I'll do it."

"I'm not going anywhere."

Damn, she was stubborn. "I'll carry you. It's not all that far."

"Five miles."

"Watch me." He snared her around the waist and hefted her.

She gasped. "Put me down, Garrett Keeley!"

With only two feet of chain between them, he couldn't lift her high enough to drape her over his shoulder. It was going to be damn awkward to carry her like this all the way into town. Squirming and beating his back with her fists, she wasn't exactly cooperating, either.

"Think a minute, Garrett. What earthly good will it do you to go after Hailey?"

"I'll be able to beat the hell out of Bud, for one thing."

"Wonderful. And how will that make Hailey feel, to have you beat up the man she loves? She'll hate you, Garrett. You don't want that. Not if you care about her."

He lowered her back to the floor. He hated smart women. Particularly those who were smarter than he was.

Odd how he'd temporarily forgotten that—along with the feel of Charity's firm body and soft breasts rubbing against him.

"Do you expect me to just let this slide? Your brother stole the woman I was going to marry right out from under my nose. You want me to turn the other cheek?"

"You're upset. I can understand that. But there are some things you simply can't change. You can't go back and undo what has happened." Pursing her lips, she glanced away, out the window toward the barns and the shelter where the pigs were kept. "Evidently Hailey and Bud love each other. I think they have for years, but her parents wouldn't let her see Bud."

"Apparently they got together long enough to plan my kidnapping."

"That's my point." She looked up at him with those soft brown eyes, sincerity shining from them. "She's made her commitment to Bud. I know it hurts to realize that. It's got to. But I don't think going after them is going to fix anything except maybe your ego. And that would only be temporary."

Was she right? he wondered. His ego had been battered pretty badly of late. Getting married to the hometown girl he'd dated off and on over the years had seemed like a reasonable thing to do while he was waiting to get his knee rehabilitated and find a new NFL team that would appreciate his quarterbacking talents. The 49ers certainly hadn't, not after he'd blown out his knee for the second time.

He snapped his thoughts away from his career and back to the question at hand. Had he only been marking time with Hailey? If that was the case, he was a worse louse than he'd thought. He cared about her, dammit! But love? Given the emotionally sterile family in which he'd grown up, maybe he wouldn't even know love if it came up and slapped him in the face.

He looked down at Charity, her body still touching his, her scent teasing his nostrils because he hadn't let her go, hadn't set her far enough away from him. Something twisted in his chest. Envy, he suspected. She'd been raised in a family, however poor, that knew how to love. He'd seen it in the way she'd looked at her brother—even in anger—remembered it from how loving the grandparents had been who had raised her.

"Okay," he said cautiously. Somewhere on this farm there had to be a hacksaw or a sledgehammer and chisel. To find them—and get himself out of this mess—he'd bide his time, lulling Charity into believing he'd bought her idea. Meanwhile he'd be patient and wait for his chance to escape. "What if I decide not to go after them? Then what?"

Lifting her shoulders, Charity exhaled the breath she'd been holding. "We'll think of something."

"Don't tell me you're all that thrilled to have us shackled together for three days."

"I won't." For reasons Garrett would never understand, and she'd never tell him, Charity didn't want to be linked to him. Besides, he was too masculine, too much of a macho playboy, too darn attractive for his own good. Or hers. And he was in love with another woman, one who was far more attractive and sophisticated than she. "We'll think of something," she repeated.

"So do we just sit here and stare at each other, for three days—"

"No. I have to—" Good Lord, how would she survive such intimate contact with Garrett for three whole days? Bud hadn't known what he was asking of her. "I've got to feed the pigs," she blurted out.

"You what?"

"This is a pig farm. Pigs eat. A lot." She took a step toward the back door but was hauled up short by the ankle bracelet. She whipped around. "Are you coming or what? This is my livelihood, you know. And Hailey just blew a really nice gig for me by canceling her wedding."

He lifted his hands in surrender. "I understand now. The pigs have a lot higher priority than I do."

"You've got that straight." She tossed the comment over her shoulder as she marched to the door. Thank goodness he kept up with her. Otherwise she would have fallen flat on her face. Again.

If the only distance she could put between herself and Garrett was two feet of chain, she'd take every inch. She owed her brother a chance at happiness. Best friends—especially when they were siblings—had to help each other out.

On the back porch, Charity reached for her heavy black rubber boots and handed another pair to Garrett. "You can wear Bud's. They ought to fit you."

"Just how do you expect us to get boots on over this chain?"

"Oh." She hadn't considered that little problem. "Well, we can each wear one, anyway."

"Nothing like making a fashion statement," he muttered, pulling a boot over his left shoe. His hip bumped against hers. "It'll probably be the rage in no time."

Her hip bumped against his. "I'm trying to make the best of a bad situation."

"Forgive me if I'm not all that cheerful. It hasn't been one of my better days."

With an odd, out-of-sync rhythm of boots and rattling chain, they clopped down the steps to the backyard.

From the front of the house, she heard a car enter the driveway.

"Hey, somebody's here," Garrett said. He grabbed her arm, half hauling her around to the side of the house. "Maybe Hailey changed her mind. Or Bud's come to his senses. I'm still going to beat the living hell out of—"

By the time they rounded the corner of the house, the car had already backed out and was turning onto the county road that fronted the property.

Standing in the middle of the driveway, his soccer uniform stained with grass and mud, was Charity's seven-year-old son, Donnie.

Charity's heart slammed against her ribs; her breath lodged in her lungs.

The boy grinned and waved. "Hi, Mom. We won! I made two goals, and Charlie Pitzer got a bloody nose." He dropped the ball he'd been holding and dribbled down the driveway toward her, expertly weaving his way past imaginary opponents.

Charity curled her fingers into her palms to keep

her hands from trembling. Bud's kidnapping escapade had created more problems for her than he ever could have guessed.

Her son was the biggest one of all.

Chapter Two

"I didn't know you had a kid." Though if Garrett had seen the boy on the street, he might have recognized those soft brown eyes and hair with so much natural curl it tended to frizz. The resemblance between the youngster and his mother was uncanny. As near as Garrett could tell, the boy's father hadn't contributed a single gene.

"Come here, Donnie. I want you to meet Mr. Keeley." In a self-conscious gesture, she shifted her braid to the front of her shoulder.

Neatly stopping the ball with his toe right beside his mother, the boy eyed Garrett warily. "Hi."

Charity hooked her arm around her son's shoulders and gave him a hug. "Mr. Keeley's going to be, ah, staying with us for a few days."

"Hello, Donnie." Garrett extended his hand, and the boy took it, the child's small hand vanishing into his larger one. The youngster's blue-and-white shirt was a mess, there were scabs on his knees and his socks drooped around his ankles. Par for the course for a kid that age. Garrett had probably looked worse. "Sounds like you're a pretty good soccer player."

"I'm a striker. Scored more than anybody else on my team last year."

"He's very athletic," Charity said, a proud smile teasing the corners of her lips. "And smart, too, aren't you, sport?" She ruffled his sweat-dampened hair.

Donnie squirmed out of reach and looked Garrett up and down.

"I play a little football myself," Garrett said. Given the fiasco of losing his bride on their wedding day, he wouldn't give himself very high marks at the moment in the intelligence department.

"Soccer's better," Donnie said with the uncompromising confidence of youth. "Not so much standin' around and lookin' dumb."

"I see." Guess that put Garrett in his place, he thought with wry amusement. The kid had a smart mouth just like his mother.

Cocking his head, Donnie eyed the links that tied his mother to Garrett. "Hey, Mom, how come you and Mr. Keeley are chained together?"

Out of the mouths of babes. A question that went right to the heart of the matter. Anxious to hear the answer himself, Garrett decided to let Charity respond.

"Your uncle Bud is playing a little trick on us. You know how he likes his practical jokes." Her forced laugh rang as phony as hell, and her smile was strained.

The boy didn't seem to notice. He shrugged. "Can I have something to eat, Mom? I'm hungry."

"Of course, honey. There's a burrito in the freezer. You can zap it in the microwave."

"Way cool!" Grinning, Donnie scooped up his ball and made a dash for the back door.

"Wash your hands before you eat," Charity called after the boy. But the kid had already vanished inside.

Garrett waited for the sound of the slamming door before he said, "At least when your husband comes home, he can take us into town and we can get these shackles taken off."

"I don't have a husband."

No husband? Currently? Or never? he wondered. "Just like you don't have a hacksaw?"

Her head snapped up. "My brother deserves a chance at happiness, Garrett. You're staying here for three days. Get used to it."

Taking her by the shoulders, he brought his face very close to hers and glared into her soft brown eyes. "Look, this was supposed to be my wedding day. Even if I don't go after Hailey, I am not going to hang around—"

Waaaaaaagggh! The awful, bloodcurdling cry came from behind him.

He turned just in time to see the biggest hog he'd ever seen in his life hurtling toward him. A thousand pounds of bacon on the hoof coming at him like a linebacker determined to chalk up a quarterback sack.

"No, Rambo!" Charity shouted.

Rambo?

Trying to elude the rush, Garrett spun around and got caught up by the chain. The hog clipped him right behind the knees. Garrett went down with a jarring crash. "Dammit!"

"Rambo, leave him alone!"

Snorting and fussing, breathing hot and heavy, the hog stuck his nose in Garrett's face. He rolled into a ball to protect himself and covered his head with his hands.

Charity whacked Rambo on the snout. "He's not hurting me, Rambo. Get off of him." Tangled in the chain, she was straddling Garrett. She lost her balance and sat down hard on his midsection.

"Auf," Garrett grunted.

The pig barked a distinctly doglike sound. But he backed off.

"Is that animal crazy? Why did he attack—?"

"He's not crazy. He's *protecting* me."

"What? He thinks he's a guard dog or something?"

"Yes. And this is *his* territory. *You* were attacking *me.*"

"I wasn't doing any such thing." But he had been, or at least Garrett could understand how a stupid pig would think that. He was also decidedly aware of Charity on top of him, her position downright suggestive. Intimate. And arousing. So much so, Garrett was glad her son was inside the house and out of view.

How many years ago had it been, that picnic at the lake? Everybody sort of pairing off after dark. He and Charity had drifted away from the others....

Charity's eyes widened and she gasped. She felt the thickening press of Garrett's arousal against the apex of her thighs. Reacted to it. Heat flooding her body. Memories. Wanting.

Ohmigod...ohmigod...ohmigod.

She scrambled to get untangled, to get away from Garrett. She made matters worse by dragging her leg across his groin. And still she couldn't get loose. Couldn't get away.

Tears of frustration burned at the backs of her eyes.

"Easy, doll." He clamped his big strong hands around her waist. "Let's take things a bit slower so you don't severely damage an important part of my anatomy."

Her face flushed hot.

Snorting, Rambo rooted at Garrett's shoulder.

"I didn't mean... It's your wedding day." *To another woman.* Aghast at what she was feeling, how she was reacting—and what he must be thinking—she wanted to find the nearest hole and crawl in. "I'm sorry."

Very gently he lifted her away so she was kneeling next to him. There was an odd look in his eyes, as though he might be remembering, too. She didn't want him to remember. Not now. Not ever. She couldn't afford him to recall what had happened so many years ago.

"See if you can call off your guard dog," he urged quietly.

She nodded. "Rambo, honey. Sweet Pea's calling you. You'd better see what's the matter." There were indeed anxious calls coming from the pig parlor. It didn't take much to get the sows excited. In their eyes, Rambo was definitely a ladies' man.

So was Garrett, Charity reminded herself. He'd had groupies following him around since he'd quarterbacked the high-school football team to a league championship. College successes had meant the same female entourage falling at his feet. Turning professional hadn't lessened his ability to attract any woman within a hundred-mile radius.

But that wasn't why, a long time ago, Charity had succumbed to his charm. Not that it mattered now.

And she wasn't planning to make the same mistake twice.

Apparently considering his work successfully completed in protecting Charity, Rambo ambled off toward the pig parlor to investigate the ruckus there.

Sitting up, Garrett rested his elbow on one bent knee and plowed his fingers through his hair. Streaks of dirt covered the front of his pleated tuxedo shirt; one diamond stud had popped out and was nowhere to be seen. With the top button missing, she could see the smooth column of his throat, a few strands of blond chest hair peeking out.

With an effort, she dragged her gaze away and searched the ground. "You've, ah, lost one of your studs."

"Don't worry about it. On top of everything else that's happened today, one stud more or less isn't going to make much difference."

He was amazingly casual about a lost diamond, she mused, but then he'd never had to pinch pennies to make ends meet.

"You were right earlier." He gave the front of his shirt a futile brush with the back of his hand. "If this situation wasn't so awful, it'd be downright funny. All in one day, I'm kidnapped, my bride runs off with some other guy and I'm attacked by the pig from hell."

"Hog. Or boar. Rambo wouldn't like to be called a pig. He'd think it was demeaning."

"He *thinks*?" Incredulously he cocked one beautifully sculpted golden brown brow.

Her lips twitched. "Haven't you heard? Pigs are very intelligent."

"Hogs."

"You're right." A nervous giggle erupted. She clamped her mouth shut.

A glint of humor appeared in his eyes. "You still want to feed those damn pigs?"

"I should at least check the feeder bins. I'm not sure Bud got them filled this morning."

"He was probably distracted."

"I'm sorry."

He studied her a minute, then cupped the back of her head. "Not your fault."

With surprising tenderness, he pulled her toward him. She hadn't expected him to kiss her, hadn't been prepared for his mouth to claim hers with hot, sensual pressure. Stunned, she couldn't have moved if her life had depended upon it. His lips were insistent, determined. So sweet she ached with the memories.

When he broke the kiss, her heart was thundering in her chest. Her breath scissored through her lungs like she'd been chasing after a whole herd of runaway pigs.

"Why did you do that?" she asked, her voice no more than a hoarse whisper.

"I didn't get to kiss the bride. I figured I deserved a consolation prize."

His words pummeled her like the sledgehammer he'd been looking for. That long-ago day of the picnic at the lake, he'd had his eye on another girl, a college coed who'd flaunted her cute little behind at him and then turned him down for an older man. Charity had been handy. And willing. His consolation prize, she supposed.

Just like now. Stinging pain rushed through her like a swarm of angry bees. But she would not let him know much his words hurt.

Lifting her chin and mentally adding a little starch to her spine, she got to her feet. "Our sows get really mean tempered if they don't get enough to eat. I suggest we get to work."

"I certainly wouldn't want Rambo to sic his whole team on me." With athletic grace, he levered himself to his feet and brushed off his black tuxedo pants. It didn't do much good. He'd gotten as much mud ground into his trousers as Donnie had on his soccer shorts.

He took a step to join her on the path to the pig parlor and winced as his knee buckled.

"What's wrong?" she asked. She reached out to steady him, but he waved her off.

"Same old thing. My knee got zinged when Rambo flattened me."

"Does it hurt much?"

He shrugged stoically. "No more than usual."

"Do you want to put some ice on it? I could ask Donnie to—"

"It's fine," he insisted.

"I heard that you won't be able to play again because of your injury."

"You heard wrong. I'm going to prove those doctors don't know what they're talking about. I'm in rehab. My knee's getting stronger every day." As if to emphasize his point, he lengthened his stride.

Charity hurried to keep up. She'd wondered how

he was coping with the loss of his career. Apparently he didn't see it that way.

"My agent's talking to a couple of teams now. I figure, with any luck at all, I ought to be wearing a uniform again by the time the season starts in September." He slanted her a glance. "Then we'll see who has the last laugh."

"I hope it works out for you." She knew how hard he'd worked to be successful in his career. It had been his whole life—outside of a string of women whose names had been linked with his. He seemed to have had plenty of time to fit them into his schedule.

The late-June sun beat down on the aluminum roof of the pig parlor, raising the temperature by several degrees even though it was an open-air facility. The pigs in the finishing pen greeted Charity with a series of pleasant *ronking* sounds as she checked their self-feeding bins.

"Hi, guys," she said in return. "Looks like Bud didn't forget you after all."

"I thought pigs liked to wallow in the mud. This place looks pretty fancy. Almost high-tech."

She glanced around at the separate pens with sloping concrete floors, automatic drinking fountains and spigots that could spray a fine mist in the air to keep the pigs cool. The installation of all this equipment had cost her far more than simply the need to pay off a bank loan. It had forced her to make a vow of secrecy she would never dare break.

"My grandfather upgraded about nine or ten years ago. Right before the floor dropped out of the price of pork. Until then the pigs did a lot of wallowing. This is much healthier for them."

He absorbed that information without comment. "I'm almost afraid to ask, but are those black things in the pen bowling balls?"

"Uh-huh. We buy them used from the bowling alley in Modesto. Pigs get bored if they don't have something to do. They're likely to bite off each other's tails."

"So they started a bowling league?" Garrett asked incredulously.

She laughed. "Maybe I ought to challenge Henderson's pig farm down the road. We could place a few bets on the side and cover the cost of transportation."

"Sounds like a winner to me." For the first time since Bud had hauled him into the house, Garrett actually smiled at her, that cocky grin she remembered so well.

A band tightened around her heart, and she had to look away.

He fell into step beside her as she headed for the nursery pen. Already they'd learned to adjust for their shackles, moving around the pig parlor like two dancers who had taken a while to sense each other's rhythms and then finally relaxed enough to simply go with the music.

Charity suspected Garrett would be a terrific dance partner. She'd seen him—strong and agile—take off with a football in his arms and run the length of the field, eluding would-be tacklers with all the grace of a ballet dancer. She'd always been amazed that such a large man, six feet two and two hundred pounds, could move with so little apparent effort.

At the nursery, she knelt to pick up one of the

piglets suckling at its mother's teats. It nuzzled into her neck, making sweet, chattering sounds.

"Isn't she beautiful," Charity said.

"Which one? Mom or her kid?"

"Both, really." The sow looked quite content with a row of her babies all suckling happily. Charity envied her total lack of worry over the future. Or the past.

"I can't say that I've ever known anyone who thought pigs were all that pretty."

"Then you've never met a hog breeder before."

Hesitantly he patted the little pig's head. "Suppose he knows he's doomed to be somebody's dinner?"

"Do any of us really know what our futures will be?"

"I guess not." He slid his hands into his pockets. In his wildest dreams he never would have foreseen a day like this one. Nor would he have thought seeing Charity hold a silly little pig in her arms would make him think of her cuddling her own baby. At one time she had, he realized. A curly-haired little boy. He kept forgetting Charity was a mother. Apparently no one in town had thought to mention it to him. Not that there would have been a reason.

She looked extraordinarily natural standing there holding a pig, and utterly feminine. He doubted that the most classic cover model wearing the most expensive, revealing gown could look any more womanly.

That revelation struck him as odd.

Charity wasn't truly beautiful. Though her hair was lustrous, it had a bizarre tendency to frizz when it escaped the braid she usually wore. And she had a slight widow's peak that on someone else wouldn't be at all attractive. On her it seemed to work. Maybe because it drew attention to her expressive eyebrows and gentle brown eyes.

Come to think of it, Garrett wouldn't mind having her cuddle with him.

Immediately he felt a flash of guilt for admiring Charity quite so blatantly. He was supposed to be marrying Hailey today. He had planned to be as good a husband as he knew how.

It looked like he wasn't going to get the chance. Still, it was too soon to be having thoughts of another woman.

"WOULD YOU LIKE something to eat?" Charity asked, tugging off the one rubber boot she'd been wearing and dropping it onto the back porch.

"Sure." Garrett held the door open for her, then followed her into the house.

She wondered if she'd ever get used to having him so close beside her. Not that she wanted to make it a habit. Instead, she'd rather have Bud cut his honeymoon short. *Very* short. "Anything in particular sound good to you?"

"A wedding buffet would be nice. Three or four salads, fresh asparagus, rice or baked potatoes, choice of prime rib or roast turkey. Whatever you'd like to whip up."

"They sure know how to do it right at the country club, don't they?" Not that Charity had ever been invited to a wedding reception there except as the official photographer. She definitely didn't run with that crowd. In contrast, Garrett's father had once been the club president, she remembered. "Would you consider a cheese-and-bologna sandwich instead?''

''That'll be fine.'' He started to sit down at the kitchen table, then realized he had to stick close to her. ''Hope the Olsons had a chance to cancel the reception. It was going to cost them a bundle.''

''They're probably stuck with the bill—and a whole lot of doggie bags.''

''Maybe they can feed the homeless with the leftovers,'' he muttered.

Taking turns, they washed up at the sink and then started on the sandwiches.

He took the bread she handed him and slathered mayonnaise and mustard on four slices. She dropped the meat and cheese in place. The TV was playing in the other room. It sounded like Donnie had found some sort of a sporting event to watch. Except that Charity and Garrett were shackled together, it all seemed very domestic. Like a family.

Which they weren't, she sternly reminded herself. She'd never had any illusions about her and Garrett getting together. It hadn't been in the cards eight years ago. And certainly wasn't now.

The agreement she'd made with Garrett's father made that out of the question.

''You want lettuce?'' she asked, tamping down the sense of regret that surfaced in spite of her best intentions.

''Sure. You got any chips?''

''In the cupboard above the mixer.''

He went in that direction; she proceeded toward the refrigerator for the lettuce. And was instantly reeled back by her ankle. Whirling, she staggered, hop-stepped and lost her balance. His own equilibrium disrupted, Garrett barely caught her before she fell.

Her face slammed into his unyielding chest, and his arms wrapped around her. He smelled of musk and pure masculinity. Beneath her palms, she could feel his heart beating. A rumble of laughter started in his chest and rolled upward until it escaped in a deep-throated chuckle.

"This is crazy, Charity. We can't even get a couple of sandwiches made without getting ourselves all tangled up." His eyes were emerald green now and filled with wicked amusement. Dimples creased both of his cheeks. "You sure you don't have a hacksaw around here someplace?"

She was about to tell him of course she had one out in the toolshed. Where else? But then she heard Donnie calling from the living room.

"Hey, Mom, somebody drove up outside. I think it's that lady from the bookstore."

"Agatha Flintstone," Charity whispered, alarmed. The owner of the town's one bookstore, as well as the city clerk, she had her pulse on the entire community and was the unofficial town crier. "Why would she—?"

"I don't much care why she's here if she's got a car." He palmed the side of Charity's head, smoothing her flyaway curls. "I think it's time we ended this charade. She can drive us into town."

"No. You don't understand." Panic rippled through Charity and mixed in a frighteningly delicious way with the erotic feel of Garrett touching her. "Agatha's the biggest gossip in all of Grazer's Corners. If she so much as *sees* you here, the word will be spread all over town in a manner of minutes after she gets home. She might even think you're the one who dumped Hailey."

"I'll be happy to explain that's not the case."

"But if Agatha gets hold of the story first, she'll get it all mixed up. Bud and Hailey will never get to explain their side. The Olsons will be embarrassed worse than just having the wedding canceled. You can't let that happen."

"Everyone will know the story eventually."

"But not yet. Not till Bud and Hailey get back," she pleaded. Lord, her brother was relying on her. The last thing he'd want would be for Agatha to be spreading tales about him.

Slowly Garrett said, "Your brother's a very lucky guy. I don't think anyone has ever loved me as much as you love him."

"Of course they have. Your parents—"

"My father wanted me to get the Heisman Trophy so much he could taste it. When I came in second in the voting, he figured I'd let him down."

Charity drew in a shocked breath. Dear heaven, she'd known so little about him eight years ago. None of his troubles, none of his hurts. "You can't mean—"

The doorbell rang.

"Mom!"

"If you answer the door," Garrett said, "that woman is sure to see me."

"I've got to. She won't go away. She's already heard Donnie, I'm sure." Fortunately Donnie would never leave a sports program on TV to open the front door knowing it was one of his mother's friends. "You can hide behind the door," she told Garrett, improvising while she half dragged him into the living room. "I won't let her in. She won't stay long if I keep her standing on the porch."

"This isn't going to work, Charity. She's sure to notice something is wrong."

"Not Agatha. She has a one-track mind."

At least Charity hoped that was the case as she opened the door. Meanwhile she reminded herself to warn Donnie not to mention Bud's little "practical joke" to anyone in town.

"Hello, dearie, I'm not catching you at a bad time, am I?" As always, Agatha's gray hair looked like she'd teased it into a rat's nest. She was wearing one of her usual homemade smocks. Today it was a cotton pansy print in purples and reds. Just the thing to attract the Norman conquerors who were so much a part of her reading fantasy.

"Well, I was, ah, trying to sort out a few things." Like her responsibilities to her brother—and her feelings about Garrett Keeley.

"Then I won't keep you a moment. Just wanted to bring the photography book by that you requested."

"Oh, you didn't have to."

Squinting, Agatha tried to peer inside through the screen door. "I know. But it came in yesterday, and I was going to give it to you today when you were in town to photograph the Hailey Olson wedding. Of course, you heard the wedding was called off."

"I heard." With an effort, Charity avoided glancing in Garrett's direction. The shackle around her ankle had never seemed so heavy or conspicuous.

"Canceled at the very last minute. Can you imagine those two young people. Whatever were they thinking about? The whole town, not to mention her parents, all excited about the event of the year. Marrying a star quarterback. Such a waste that they would run off like that. Such a waste.''

''Yes, I suppose that's true.'' Charity opened the screen slightly. ''Did you want me to pay you now for the book?''

''Oh, no, dearie, that can wait till you're in town. I just knew how anxious you were for the book and I didn't want to make you wait.''

She'd also wanted to find out what, if anything, Charity knew about the day's events, she suspected. ''That was very thoughtful of you.''

''I don't suppose you know where that Olson girl and her beau have run off to, do you?''

''I haven't talked to Hailey since she arranged for me to take the photos,'' Charity hedged.

''Well, yes, I suppose you wouldn't know, then.'' Agatha finally passed the book to Charity. It was a heavy one and fairly technical. ''I guess I should be going. I thought maybe...well, your brother used to—''

''Bud isn't here. I don't know when he'll be back.''

''Of course, dearie. Well, toodle-loo.'' She waved her fingers in Charity's direction. ''Enjoy the book.''

''I will. Thanks for bringing it by.''

As soon as Agatha stepped off the porch, Charity closed the door and collapsed against the wall. Her eyes locked on Garrett's.

''You have talents I never suspected,'' he said.

She raised questioning brows.

''You can lie without blinking an eye.''

Chapter Three

"A few more minutes, Donnie, and then it's your bedtime." Charity kept her finger on her place in the photography book she'd been reading. Not that she hadn't already read the same paragraph three times. She still didn't know what it said.

"Aw, Mom. Garrett and me have got to finish this game first."

"That's why I'm warning you now. When the game is over, you're off to bed. You've stayed up too late as it is." Largely because Charity had wanted her son's presence as a chaperon.

Donnie scrunched his face into a scowl but he didn't directly challenge her authority. He and Garrett had been playing checkers since they'd finished a dinner of spaghetti, salad and garlic bread several hours ago.

So far Garrett was down two games to one. He was trying to even the score with this final game.

He jumped one of Donnie's red pieces and smiled grimly. There were four black pieces still left on the board versus seven remaining red ones.

Of necessity, Charity was sitting at the oak dining table with them, all too close to Garrett. He'd rolled up the sleeves of his white shirt, baring muscular arms covered with a light matting of sandy blond hair. His hands were large, the backs crossed with an assortment of scars that marked him as a professional athlete.

At dinner she'd been struck by how easily her son and Garrett had fallen in together, as if at some instinctive level they had recognized each other. How would they feel if they knew the truth? she wondered.

A shudder of apprehension went through her. She couldn't let that happen.

Bud had been Donnie's father figure since her grandfather died. She'd been comfortable with that arrangement. Until now.

Guilt niggled at her conscience. Perhaps she'd done both Donnie and Garrett a disservice. But she'd had no other choice. Not really.

Donnie double-jumped Garrett, his smile as smug as Garrett's had been grim.

"This kid's too good," Garrett complained.

"I learned from my great-grandpa," Donnie told him proudly. "He used to let me beat him, and then he got too old. So I let him beat me some."

"You're all heart, kid."

Charity smiled at the exchange. Both of them played the game as if their lives depended upon the outcome. Talk about a competitive spirit! A genetic trait, no doubt.

She was still troubled by Garrett's earlier comment about lying. The cynicism in his voice had made her wonder if he'd had a bad experience somewhere along the way—perhaps with a woman.

On the whole, she thought of herself as honest.

Lies, she knew, complicated a person's life. As far as she could recall, throughout her adult life she'd only told one lie. A big one of omission.

She had the troubling feeling it was about to catch up with her.

Garrett maneuvered his checker out of harm's way. Or so he thought. Three moves later, Donnie had both of Garrett's remaining pieces trapped in a corner.

"What kind of brain pills have you been feeding this kid?" Garrett lifted his hand and gave her son a high five. "Good job, Donnie. I'll get you next time."

"Off you go, son. And don't forget to brush your teeth."

"Yeah, yeah. I know." He hopped down from his chair. "See ya tomorrow, Garrett. If you want, I'll teach ya how to dribble a soccer ball. Coach says I'm the best dribbler around."

"That'd be great."

In spite of his much touted soccer skills, Donnie was not always light on his feet. He thundered down the hallway to his bedroom.

"No modesty there, huh?" Garrett commented with a smile.

Giving up her photography book as a waste of effort, she set it on the table. "I think a child should feel confident about his abilities."

"I wasn't kidding when I said he's smart. Does he get that from you? Or his father?"

"Both, I imagine."

He opened her book and flipped to the title page. A slight frown pleated his forehead. "If I asked you who Donnie's father is, would you tell me?"

Her stomach did the equivalent of a high dive off a thousand-foot cliff in the Sierras.

"No," she said, recovering from the plunge. She couldn't tell him. She'd promised a long time ago never to reveal that information. Particularly to Garrett.

"None of my business, huh?"

"That's right."

"Okay." He leaned back in his chair and studied her, the look in his green eyes unreadable. "So what do we do now?"

Good lord! Did he know? Or even suspect the truth? "I d-don't know what you mean," she stammered.

"I mean, do you want to take me on in a game of checkers? Or should we watch TV?"

"Oh." She nearly fell out of her chair with relief. "I guess we could watch TV." She wouldn't be able to concentrate for a minute on a checkers game—not with Garrett as her opponent.

"Great. Have you got a satellite dish?"

"Not at the prices they charge for one. My budget doesn't have a lot of room for extras."

He looked surprised. "You support yourself entirely from the pig farm?"

"Bud pays most of the household bills from his job at the candy factory." And that source of income might now be in jeopardy, she realized with a start. Garrett's father owned the place. He was unlikely to be pleased one of his employees had eloped with his son's intended bride.

She swallowed hard. "And I work part-time for the *Grazer Gazette* taking photos of newsworthy items like the garden-club ladies, new babies. That sort of thing. Plus any wedding jobs or portrait work I can get. And I've got the contract for Grazer Unified High's annual and senior pictures. That pays some of the bills."

"The pig farm doesn't turn a profit?"

"Not much."

"Then why don't you dump it?"

"This is my home, Garrett. It's where I was raised. In spite of how you or others might feel about pigs, I love living here." Charity's mother, on the other hand, had had a far different view. She'd been more than eager to get out of town as fast as she could. And look where it had gotten her. Into a relationship with a man who'd left her to raise two young children alone with no way to support herself, and without a lick of good sense. She'd nearly starved. They all had. And then she'd put her children, her own flesh and blood, on a bus for Grazer's Corners and proceeded to vanish. She'd turned up later. In a morgue.

The memories tightened in Charity's throat, and she swallowed hard, fighting back tears of abandonment as painful as those she'd shed almost twenty years ago.

Garrett's fingers tapped a restless beat on the tabletop. "Have you given any thought to our sleeping arrangements tonight? For my *wedding* night," he mocked.

His question—out of the blue—nearly drove the air from her lungs.

No, she hadn't considered that small detail.

Dammit all! If Garrett didn't kill Bud when he got back home, she just might do it herself—beloved brother or not.

Sleeping with Garrett Keeley was the last thing on earth she wanted to do.

NOT FOR THE FIRST TIME that day, Charity was totally mortified.

The chain that linked her to Garrett was barely long enough to allow some small bit of privacy in the bathroom. Of course, she couldn't close the door all the way. Nor could he when it was his turn.

Sighing, she slipped her nightgown on over her head. The oversize T-shirt came to her knees, the most modest sleeping attire she owned and far too warm for a summer evening. But any other choice would be beyond foolish.

She gave her hair one last stroke with the brush and opened the door. "Your turn."

With an amused smile, he looked her over, starting at the top of her head and moving slowly, leisurely downward, lingering on her breasts—making her nipples pebble—and taking in the sacklike fit of her gown. Her flesh heated under his intense scrutiny.

"Mother Hubbard, I take it."

"I didn't think a suit of armor would be required to protect my honor."

His lips quirked. "Trust me on this, sweetheart. If I decided to enjoy my *honeymoon* with you, you'd enjoy it, too. You'd be shedding whatever you were wearing faster than I could—"

"You wouldn't!" He was teasing her. She hoped.

"Haven't you heard? Honor has never been my strong suit."

She'd heard the stories all right; she hadn't always

wanted to believe them. "But you wouldn't force yourself on a woman."

He leaned against the doorjamb and shook his head. His eyes darkened as he perused her again. "I've never had to—and you damn well know it."

That was a good reminder—as good as a slap across the face. He hadn't forced her into anything she hadn't wanted eight years ago.

She squared her shoulders. That wasn't going to happen again. "I'll get you a pair of Bud's pajamas. They ought to fit."

"I prefer to sleep nude."

Her eyes widened, and forbidden images popped into her head. Fascinatingly masculine images.

"Unfortunately, with this shackle around my ankle, I won't be able to get my pants off."

"What a pity," she said dryly.

"I knew you'd be disappointed."

What she was was a nervous wreck.

By the time they got into bed, her mouth was dry and her heart was beating like she had a severe case of old-maid palpitations. She could barely draw a steady breath.

He was impossibly large in her double bed, his broad shoulders and enticingly bare chest taking up far more than his half of the space. Her mind kept cycling over the awareness that this was—or should have been—his wedding night.

And the foolish, impossible fantasy of *her* being his bride.

She squeezed her eyes shut to block out the persistent images she mentally snapped with the camera of her imagination.

Leaning on his elbow, Garrett looked down at

Charity. She certainly wasn't the woman he'd expected to share his bed with tonight. The fact that Hailey had obviously been lying to him for the past several months grated on him more than he cared to admit. He'd been honest with Hailey. *Honorable,* as Charity would say. He and Hailey had known each other a long time, off and on since high school; he'd thought their relationship was easy, comfortable. Maybe too easy. Not enough zing to last until the wedding day.

Damn, he'd never figure out women.

He still didn't know why Charity hadn't returned his phone calls after that night at the lake. He'd tried several times to reach her. He'd never gotten any further than leaving a message with her grandfather.

He frowned. "You did know I tried to call you?"

Her eyes opened slowly, and she focused on his face. "When was that?"

Like she didn't remember? And he'd thought the sex had been pretty damn good. "After the picnic. At the lake. You never called back."

"Oh." She tugged the sheet up to her chin. "I can't remember. I guess I got busy."

"Yeah. Right." With the backs of his knuckles, he skimmed a path down her cheek. Warm, soft velvet with the scent of cinnamon. "If you've forgotten, maybe I ought to try to help you remember. You aren't busy now, are you?"

"Very. I'm trying to sleep." Her quick intake of air that raised the sheet over her breasts suggested she wasn't entirely immune to his touch. "Why don't you turn off the light?"

He ignored her suggestion. "It wouldn't take long." He let his thumb drag across her lips. The lower one was slightly pouty and very kissable. "Maybe an hour."

"An hour?" Her voice cracked.

"Longer if you'd like."

"No!" She tried to scoot away from him, but of course she couldn't. Not the way they were shackled together.

To emphasize her inability to escape, he tugged her leg over to his side of the bed. She jerked it back where it had been.

He chuckled. "I think this is going to be a very long night for both of us. We could make it a pleasant one." The fact was, in this compromising position, Garrett was becoming aroused. He hadn't intended to. It was just a game, teasing her. His libido seemed to think otherwise.

She flopped onto her side, her back to him, and curled into a ball. Like a golden brown waterfall, her hair draped over the pillow.

Lowering his head, he placed a kiss beneath her ear. Such a small, delicate ear, he mused, the swirls perfectly formed like a fragile seashell.

"Garrett...don't."

"If I'm making you uncomfortable, maybe you ought to tell me where the hacksaw is. Then we can both end our misery."

He thought for a moment she was going to give in—or else roll over and make love with him. Instead, a single tear escaped from the corner of her eye.

"I can't, Garrett. My brother..." Her throat worked convulsively. "Besides Donnie, he's the only family I have. He's counting on me."

Aw, hell!

Garrett flopped onto his back, causing the bed to creak, and stared up at the ceiling. It was white and had a maze of tiny cracks running through it like the paint was old or the house had been shaken by one too many California earthquakes. How the hell was he supposed to deal with Charity's stubborn loyalty?

And how the hell was he going to lie here all night next to her and *not* make love to her? He'd never claimed to be a saint. Given the way he'd been stood up at the altar, he was as free of obligations as the next man.

Except Charity had given him the brush-off.

First his bride. Now his bedmate.

Days didn't get any worse than this!

THE NIGHT SOUNDS DRIFTED in the open window, a chorus of crickets chirping and frogs croaking at the pond that lay at the edge of the property. But all Charity could hear was Garrett's steady breathing.

She'd been listening for hours.

No way could she go to sleep. Not with him in her bed.

He would never know how much she had wanted him to make love to her. The lonely ache she'd ignored for years had exploded into a painful throbbing deep in her midsection, racking her body with a need she'd denied but couldn't quite forget.

He wasn't the man for her. She'd known that eight years ago. Nothing had changed. Even if they hadn't had a past, there wouldn't be a future for them.

Unlike Hailey, she wouldn't be accepted by his family and wouldn't fit into his career. She was as far from the trophy wives pro athletes sported on their arms as a woman could be. A pig farmer! She could hear the sports commentators now. Talk about proving to be an embarrassment.

And her son. Where would Donnie fit into Garrett's life? Douglas Keeley, Garrett's father, had already rejected the idea that any relationship existed. She'd agreed. The deal was notarized and in writing—with penalty clauses.

She closed her eyes against her burning tears and swallowed a sob. She'd committed the ultimate betrayal of her son's birthright. She'd had to. For the love of her family.

The next thing she knew, the sun was glancing off the top of the bedroom window and the heavy weight of a man's arm rested across her middle.

Her eyes flew open. She was spooned against Garrett, her bottom nestled against his firm and very obvious arousal. Her whole body reacted in an instant. Wanting. Needing. Melting into him.

Groaning, she jerked away.

He wouldn't let her go.

"Sweetheart, you're killing me. If I swear I won't leave the farm till Bud gives the okay, you suppose we could find some way to get these shackles off?"

"Yes." The word came out as a hoarse croak. If she had to, she'd cut off her own foot to escape the one thing she wanted more than life and could never have.

"DONNIE, I'VE TOLD YOU not to ride Rambo like that."

Straddling the pig like a cowboy riding a bronco,

the youngster swatted the animal's rump with his baseball cap. "He doesn't care."

Charity rolled her eyes. "He's hopeless."

"I'd say he was all boy." Standing some distance away, Garrett raised his leg and planted his foot on a low rock wall that surrounded a small flower garden. It felt strange not to be attached to Charity. They hadn't gotten rid of the cuffs but at least they'd been able to snap the chain on both ends. The bolt cutter that had been in the toolshed all along had worked just fine.

"More likely he's showing off for you." She hefted a wheelbarrow filled with grain sacks and pushed it toward the pigpens.

"Let me," Garret said.

"I can manage."

"I know. But it hurts the male chauvinist pig in me to watch you work while I'm standing around doing nothing." He'd found a short-sleeved shirt in Bud's closet to wear, though it looked damn odd with his tuxedo pants. Charity was wearing faded denim jeans and a blouse she'd tied up around her middle. He tried not to think about how her bare skin would feel.

Relinquishing her grip on the wheelbarrow, she stepped out of his way.

"I thought Bud was in charge of feeding the pigs," Garrett said.

"He handles it on the weekends. During the week, he's got to be at work pretty early, so it's my job."

Charity wasn't a particularly delicate woman. But Garrett didn't like the idea of her having to do so much physical work. She ought to be pampered, not worn to a nub by farm work. ''Guess your grandparents have passed on?''

''Uh-huh.'' She indicated he should stop by the pen with the sow and her babies. ''Gramps had a stroke about eight years ago. After that he couldn't do much of the work himself, and Grandma had her hands full trying to take care of him. Bud and I pretty well took over running the farm then. You get used to it.''

''You couldn't have been very old.''

She ripped open one of the feed sacks. ''That was my senior year at Grazer Unified.''

As Garrett recalled, Charity had just been entering her senior year at high school that time at the picnic. She'd been one of the youngest kids in the crowd. Facing his own senior year at college, he'd seen her around town a time or two, and had been drawn to her that day. He wasn't quite sure why. There'd been prettier girls at the picnic. College coeds who fawned over him and the chance that he might win the Heisman Trophy. Charity hadn't seemed all that impressed with football.

He grinned. Her son wasn't, either. Soccer was Donnie's game. Or playing cowboy on a pig.

''You could have sold the place when your grandfather couldn't handle the work anymore,'' Garrett said, taking the feed sack away from her to pour the contents into a feeding bin.

''He would have died if he'd been forced to leave. His grandfather settled this part of the country before the Grazers ever thought about coming west.''

''I thought the Grazers founded the town.''

''That's what they'd like everyone to believe.'' She gave a toss of her long hair, which she'd pulled back and looped around on itself. "The Ardens know better."

He chuckled. The Grazers had always been a little uppity, demanding their due at Founders' Day events and touting their daughter, Jordan, as better than anybody else in town. Despite her parents, Jordan hadn't quite bought into all the hype. She was a good kid. He hoped to goodness no great harm had come to her at the hands of the man who'd kidnapped her from her own wedding on a motorcycle. The guy had looked vaguely familiar....

"At any rate, Gramps died two years ago. Six months later, Grandma went. She'd been in failing health, and I think she was so lonely without him, she simply didn't want to go on living."

"So you carried the burden of running this place and taking care of your grandparents on your own for all those years?" She'd barely been more than a kid, Garrett realized, and had her own child to raise.

"Bud does his share. And without his job at the factory, we never would have made it. He gave up an agricultural engineering degree to stay home."

Garrett had emptied one bag of feed and shouldered the next one. "I'm impressed."

"Don't be. When our mother got tired of playing at being a parent, Gramps and Grandma took us in without blinking an eye. Frankly it was the best thing that could have happened to us."

That revelation rocked Garrett back on his heels. He'd never given any thought to why she'd been living with her grandparents. Now he suspected there was an ugly side to her past. And that she was a survivor.

As they worked around the pigpens, Garrett's admiration for Charity's strength and determination intensified. This was hard work, particularly for a woman. Even his shoulders were beginning to feel the strain, and except for his knee, he was in top shape. Meanwhile the pigs were happily smacking and munching and grunting, opening and slamming the lids to their feeders, and generally making a whole lot of noise. He'd always thought it was supposed to be quiet in the country.

"You'd better take a rest," she said. "I'll finish up."

"I'm fine. What's next?" With his forearm, he wiped the sweat away from his forehead.

"Your knee is beginning to bother you."

He scowled at her. "What makes you think that?"

"You've started to limp. Sit down and rest it."

"It's better if I keep moving."

Shaking her head, she muttered something about men having to be so darn macho.

Evidently she'd never heard the expression "No pain, no gain." Or had a coach who didn't know the meaning of the word *quit*.

Garrett followed her into an area where two sows huge with pregnancy were waiting in separate stalls for their labor to start.

"I thought every pig farm was required to have its own border collie," he commented.

She turned and smiled, a warm smile filled with humor. "I'll bet you saw *Babe*," she teased.

"I've been waiting for the pigs to start talking to me."

"You're just not listening. They talk all the

time.'' Reaching into a pen, Charity petted the snout of one of the sows. The pig responded with a couple of friendly oinks. ''Donnie's allergic to dog and cat hair. That's why he turned Rambo into his pet. In fact, if we aren't careful, Rambo begins thinking he's a dog and comes right on in the house.''

''I'm allergic, too.''

She straightened and shot him a look. ''I didn't know that.''

He shrugged. ''Lots of people are. It's no big deal. Except when I was a kid I used to drive my parents crazy asking for a dog. The best I ever did was get a guinea pig for my sixth birthday.'' He remembered thinking he'd rather have had a dog and gotten rid of his asthmatic reaction, but his parents had assured him that wasn't a choice. Maybe he should have asked his folks for a real pig instead.

''Hey, Garrett!'' Donnie came running into the pig shed. ''Aren't you done yet? I was gonna teach you how to dribble.''

''I'll be right with you, kid.''

''Go ahead,'' Charity said.

''If you're sure...''

She waved him off. ''Try not to twist your knee. I don't want to be responsible if you damage yourself again.''

Unreasonably he felt a little piqued at her comment. He wasn't a child. Getting back to his career was the most important thing he could think of. He wouldn't risk that. So what if he got a few twinges now and then? *No pain, no gain.*

He and Donnie played around for a while, the youngster doing most of the work and all of the showing off. After about a half hour, a station wagon appeared, pulling off the road into the Ardens' driveway.

Wondering if the time had come for him to move on, Garrett asked Donnie, "Who's that?"

"Huh?" The boy looked up after he drove the ball between two fence posts he had designated as the goal. "Oh, that's Homer. He's the butcher at Grazer's Groceries."

"You get your meat delivered?"

"Sometimes he brings stuff. Mostly he's my mom's boyfriend."

The shock of that announcement sent adrenaline surging through Garrett's body with such power he could have kicked Donnie's soccer ball clear into the next county.

Chapter Four

Charity felt the animosity all the way from the far side of the pig parlor. Garrett had taken on a wide-legged, aggressive stance, his fists clenched at his side, and looked a lot like Rambo did when he was being protective of his sows.

Poor Homer looked like he was about to cut and run. Or pass out.

She hurried across the yard to intervene before any serious damage was done.

"Hi, Homer," she said, intentionally stepping between the two men. Donnie appeared oblivious to what was going on, his mind occupied with practicing his left-footed dribble. "What brings you out this way?"

"I, ah, tried to call." His gaze darted past her to Garrett. "I didn't mean to interrupt anything."

"You're not, Homer." By way of introduction, she gestured vaguely toward the man standing behind her. "Garrett is an acquaintance of Bud's."

"An acquaintance your brother kidnapped," Garrett muttered under his breath.

Nervously Homer shifted his weight from one foot to the other. His clean white T-shirt hung straight down on his slim frame and was neatly tucked into khaki work slacks. "Your phone's out of order."

"Really?" she said with feigned innocence, knowing full well Bud had cut the line. "I'll have to let the phone company know. Would you like to, ah, come in for a cup of coffee or ice tea?"

"He would not," Garrett said from behind her.

Unable to hear the remark, Homer shot Garrett another cautious look. "No, no, that's all right. I was just going to ask if you wanted to go into Modesto with me Saturday night. If you're not busy, I mean. The summer theater group is putting on *Arsenic and Old Lace.* I thought you might like..."

"I'd love to, Homer."

Garrett snarled a derisive comment, which Charity ignored.

"Thank you for asking me," she said.

"Great." Homer backed up a step or two. "Really great. Maybe we could all have dinner first. The girls could baby-sit Donnie while we're—"

"I don't need any darn ol' *girls* baby-sitting me!" Donnie complained, suddenly interjecting himself in the conversation.

"Smart kid," Garrett muttered.

"We'll talk about it later," she told her son.

"Well, I don't," the boy insisted, sailing the ball toward the flower beds.

Charity winced as her snapdragons took a beating.

Homer retreated another step. "Want me to call the phone company for you?"

"That's very thoughtful of you, Homer. Yes, I'd appreciate you letting them know there's trouble with the line." She also wondered what the repairman would do when he found the line had been cut. Maybe she could tell him she'd nicked it with her pruning shears. Damn, but she wished Bud would get home. And he wasn't likely to be back before tomorrow night, at the earliest. That conjured up a whole bushel of possibilities with Garrett spending another night in her home—possibilities she didn't want to consider. Thank goodness they'd done away with the chain that had bound them.

"Well, ah... Talk to you later." With an anxious wave Homer opened his car door. A moment later, he was in full retreat, backing down the driveway and out onto the highway in a cloud of dust.

"Why didn't you tell me you had a boyfriend?"

At Garrett's angry tone, she turned. His eyes were narrow slits, his lips a grim, censorious line. If she didn't know better, she would have thought... But that wasn't possible.

"I've been out with Homer a couple of—"

"We *slept* together," he hissed. "You and me! I had a right to know."

She blanched and looked quickly around to see where Donnie was and to make sure he couldn't hear their conversation. "We didn't *sleep* the way you mean it. Nothing happened."

He caught her chin between his thumb and forefinger. "We came damn close. Trust me on that, cinnamon girl." His voice was rough and raspy, unfairly intimate.

"Cinnamon?" she gasped in a whisper.

"That's how you smell. Spicy and sexy and as domestic as warm sugared toast in the morning."

She trembled, her insides churning, and shook her head. "No."

"Besides he's too old for you. He's gotta be at least forty."

"Thirty-nine."

"He's so old, he's going bald, for God's sake. The man could practically be your father."

Angry, frightened by the emotions that roiled through her, she jerked her head away from his grasp. "I'll have you know, Mr. High-and-Mighty, Homer Smith is a very fine man. He's a widower with two lovely young girls—twelve and fourteen—"

"They're probably driving him crazy and he wants some sucker to help him survive their teenage years."

"He has a steady job," she countered.

"Terrific. Give the man a balloon."

"Not everyone can get a million-dollar contract for throwing some silly ball back and forth and nearly getting himself killed by three-hundred-pound bullies landing on him every week." Unaccountably tears burned in her eyes. Anger, she told herself, did that to a woman. *Not* wanting. *Not* any other emotion she refused to acknowledge even to herself. "I'd take a nice steady, hardworking family man over a playboy jock any day of the week, *Sundays* included."

He went very still. So still, Charity thought he might be about to explode. She'd hurt his pride, slammed the career he'd chosen, the one that had made him famous—the one that caused her to worry incessantly that he'd be seriously hurt with more than a knee injury. Desperately she wanted to yank her words back, but once spoken there was no way to retrieve them.

"Good decision, cinnamon girl." He spoke so softly, so tautly she could barely hear him. "I always suspected you were smarter than most of the women I've met."

With that he turned and walked away.

Her knees were so rubbery, it was all Charity could do not to sink to the ground. But she wouldn't show weakness. Not to Garrett. Not to anyone. Her mother had been weak, particularly when it came to men. Charity had vowed never to make that same mistake.

She'd only slipped once.

GARRETT'S KNEE ACHED like hell, throbbing with each step he took across the fallow ground east of the pig barn. The doctor had warned him not to put too much stress on the joint or the damage might become irreparable. Hefting those bags of feed had not been a smart idea.

Coming to a halt, he jammed his hands into his pockets. If he didn't think it would totally ruin his chances of returning to the NFL, he'd damn well walk all the way into town.

But that would be a stupid move. Almost as dumb as the way he'd acted with Charity.

He had no claim on her, no exclusive rights. If she wanted to hang around with a butcher, so be it. He should have kept his mouth shut.

His lips quirked into a wry grin. She sure knew how to put a man in his place. She'd cut him off at the knees as neatly as a cut-back block on a charging lineman. And he'd deserved it.

He exhaled a long breath. The Arden property wasn't big—no more than a dozen acres, he supposed, half planted in corn. But it was a long way to the next farmhouse.

That's when he spotted Donnie sitting under an old oak tree, its branches gnarled and spreading outward in all directions. The kid looked as glum as Garrett felt. He limped in that direction.

"What's going down, sport?"

The kid lifted narrow shoulders. "I dunno."

Garrett kept his distance, not wanting to spook the boy, choosing a jagged outcropping of rock to sit on a few feet away from Donnie. They sat there in silence for a while, Garrett making a big deal about studying a fist-size rock he'd picked up.

"I don't want Mom to marry that *wuss,*" Donnie said.

That news hit Garrett in the midsection like a body blow. "Homer, you mean?"

"Yeah."

"Your mom told you she was going to marry him?"

"Naw. But Uncle Bud didn't say nothing about gettin' married, neither."

Garrett relaxed ever so slightly. Maybe it wasn't a done deal. Not that it was any of his business. Except he'd slept with her. For real. Eight years ago and he still remembered. "Your mother told you about Bud getting married, huh?"

"This morning. While you was shaving."

"Ah." Garrett nodded. He admired Charity for broaching the subject before Bud got home. Better to prepare the boy than to be faced with an awkward moment.

"Mom said some lady would probably come live with us and be my new aunt."

"Her name's Hailey. She's very nice. Pretty, too. You'll like her." Funny how Garrett couldn't dredge up any emotions, sad or otherwise, over his runaway bride coming back here to live with another man. He had thought he was in love with Hailey. Evidently he'd either been wrong—or incredibly blind to her real feelings and his own.

"I don't like girls."

"Yeah, well, maybe you ought to give her a chance. Homer, too, if that's who your mom wants." God, he nearly choked on the thought.

"I'm not gonna go live with Homer and those dorky girls," Donnie insisted, jutting out his lower lip. In spite of his show of bravado, his chin trembled. "I'll run away first."

The boy's threat propelled Garrett to his feet. He crossed the distance to the boy and sat down beside him. "No, you won't."

"I will so."

"Your mom needs you. Even if she marries Homer—" Involuntarily Garrett's teeth clenched, and his stomach knotted. Charity couldn't be that stupid. Besides, Garrett would kill the guy first. "—you're still her number-one man."

Donnie looked up at him with big brown eyes, stubborn replicas of Charity's softer eyes. "I am?"

"You bet, sport. She wouldn't be able to make it without you. *Numero uno!*" He ruffled the boy's coffee-brown hair, thick and curly like his mom's with golden highlights. God, where was the kid's old man? He had to be a real jerk to desert a boy like Donnie—and a woman like Charity. Or was there more to the story than she was telling?

Donnie smiled a little. "Yeah, Mom always says I'm a big help to her."

"Count on it, sport."

They did a high five, and Garrett felt a little better about himself. At least he hadn't let the kid run off on his own.

But the fact was, Homer Smith was all that Garrett wasn't. The butcher was steady and safe, a family man, probably boring, but some women didn't care. Charity included. Garrett wished that didn't bother him so much.

He did know, however, it was time for him to move on. No way could his libido handle another night in such close proximity to Charity even if they weren't sharing the same bed.

Leaving Donnie on his own—and in a more upbeat mood than when Garrett had found him—Garrett went in search of a means of transportation to get him away from the farm.

He found Charity's car in an old barn, the weather-worn planks warped so badly the sun streamed in through the gaps in the wall. The place smelled of grease and dirt. An old workbench was covered with tools, and an assortment of replacement fan belts hung on the wall. A small tractor was parked at the opposite end of the barn along with plowing discs and harvesting equipment.

Garrett popped the hood on a compact car that was about four years old.

One look told him Bud had yanked the coil wire from the distributor cap. No way to crank over the engine without one of those.

Looking around the barn, he wondered if Bud had

taken the damn thing with him on his honeymoon. That would be just his luck.

Starting with the workbench, he explored the barn in search of a coil wire and came up empty. In a room off to the side of the main building, he discovered a well-equipped darkroom. Standing there, the pungent scent of developer still lingering in the air, he studied the photos on the wall. Clearly Charity had talent. She'd turned pigs of all shapes and sizes into things of beauty; wildflowers and scenes of the Sierra foothills leaped off the wall in such vivid colors Garrett had to resist the urge to reach out and touch them, sure he'd be able to feel the texture of the floral petals and pine needles.

But it was the photos of her son that truly took his breath away. So much love radiated through the camera lens in both directions that the images touched Garrett's heart, as well as his eyes. The pictures should have been on display in a gallery, not a made-over tack room.

Given his background—his stern, rigid, unemotional parents—it was hard to imagine even ten percent of the motherly love Charity managed to communicate in a single photograph.

Maybe his reaction to Charity wasn't simply lust, he mused. Maybe it was her powerful aura of love that he could feel even when it wasn't directed at him that had him wanting to get as close to her as a man could.

Not that it mattered. She'd made it clear jocks were not high on her list of possible suitors.

Dammit all! Playing ball was all he knew how to do. All he'd ever wanted to do.

Hands in his pockets, he wandered back into the

barn and stopped in front of the green-and-yellow tractor. On a hunch, he climbed up on the seat and smiled.

Bud had evidently been in a big hurry to elope with his bride. He hadn't considered a perfectly good contingency plan for Garrett's escape. He planned to take advantage of that oversight.

CHARITY DROPPED a spoonful of pickle relish into the chopped ham, added some mayonnaise and stirred the sandwich mix. There wasn't much milk left in the refrigerator and less than a full loaf of bread in the bread box. If Bud didn't get home pretty soon, they'd be on short rations.

As she looked up, her breath caught at the sight of Garrett coming out of the barn. He was limping a little, his measured steps less swaggering than usual. She pursed her lips. What she'd said to him earlier had not only been mean. It had been a lie. Purely a defensive measure.

She'd known from the beginning there'd be no place for her in the life of a man like Garrett. Wealthy. Handsome and sexy beyond belief. A celebrity both on and off the football field, he had beautiful women fawning all over him at every opportunity. So she'd tried not to even consider the possibility, had told herself that she wouldn't want that kind of life even if there'd been a chance.

But she'd never meant for her words to be cruel.

The back door swung open with a creak of the hinges.

Concentrating on her sandwich-making task—or pretending to—she didn't look up. "I'll have lunch ready in a minute. Hope you don't mind ham-salad sandwiches. The pantry shelves are getting a little bare."

After a pause while her heart seized with emotions she wasn't about to admit, he said, "No problem. I'll just wash up."

He walked away and she exhaled. She should have apologized. Right then. But she couldn't get the words past the lump in her throat.

"Charity!" he called from the bathroom. "I think we've got a little problem in here."

"What now?" she muttered, grabbing a towel to wipe her hands. The plumbing had probably backed up and—

She came to an abrupt halt at the doorway.

"Oh, Rambo," she groaned. "You silly goose! How'd you get in here?"

"Does he take baths often?" Garrett asked mildly.

He quirked an eyebrow toward Rambo, whose snout rested on one end of the claw-foot tub, his tail curling at the other end, a decided smirk of pleasure on his face. Water had spilled over the sides of the tub and puddled on the linoleum floor.

She sighed. "Only on hot summer days when someone forgets to lock a gate."

"Looks like he's waiting for somebody to scrub his back." Garrett's lips twitched with the threat of a smile.

Charity struggled to squelch a giggle. The damn pig thought he was a lapdog. "Not a chance. When it comes to baths around here, it's strictly do-it-yourself."

"What a shame. And here I'd been hoping you'd consider—"

"Come on, help me get this big lummox out of the tub." The image of her scrubbing Garrett's muscular, bare back had popped instantly to mind, flushing her face and making her heart kick in with an extra beat. Not a good image to harbor.

She took Rambo by the ears and tugged; Garrett shoved from the rear end.

The hog grunted a series of *wheenks* in objection. Apparently he wasn't through with this bath quite yet.

"Get out, Rambo. This is a people tub."

"How did he get the water turned on?" Garrett asked mildly.

"He's got a very talented snout." She pulled again; Garrett hefted the back end. Her feet slipped on the wet floor, and she came close to going down on her butt. Rambo didn't budge.

"How 'bout trying a sharp stick at my end of the beast?" Garrett suggested. "That might get his attention."

She eyed the hog. He could be stubborn when he wanted to. Like now. "Only as a last resort. His hide's pretty thick."

"If he were mine, he'd be bacon by now."

As if he understood the threat, Rambo gave a cry like wet hands wrenching a balloon.

"He's sired a half-dozen blue-ribbon winners. Best porkers in a three-county area."

Garrett changed his position and tried to wrap his arms around Rambo's middle. "All I see is a big mess of pork chops," he said between clenched teeth. "Southern fried."

Wheeeiii. Loudly making his objections known,

Rambo scrambled with all four feet against the slippery porcelain tub.

"Ham steak is sounding better and better."

Garrett hoisted the middle; Charity pulled.

"Pickled pigs feet," Garrett grunted threateningly.

That did it.

In a panic, Rambo lumbered out of the tub, knocking Charity down and hauling Garrett halfway across the bathroom before he could let go. Squealing, the hog ran through the house and out the screen door onto the back porch without bothering to open the door.

Stunned, Charity lay on the floor trying to catch her breath. She was soaked top to bottom, and her hip stung where she'd landed on it with a whack. "Pigs feet?" she gasped, laughing. "I'll have to...remember that."

"Dried pigs ears for dogs to chew on was gonna be my next threat."

Sprawled next to her, Garrett raised himself up on his elbows. The golden flecks in his hazel eyes were dancing with amusement. A shock of his hair had slipped across his forehead and made a wet curl that clung to his skin. "It's called intimidation. I learned the technique from a couple of really good pass rushers."

She sobered instantly. "I'm sorry about what I said earlier. There's nothing wrong with being a football player."

"Except it doesn't count as a steady job?"

"I didn't mean that. It's just that when I used to see them...all those big guys making a beeline for you. And then you'd go down..."

"You watched me play?"

"On TV sometimes."

"I'm flattered."

"I didn't watch often. I was so afraid you'd be hurt and I didn't want to see—" She stopped before she said entirely too much, before she gave herself away.

He touched her cheek with his fingertips, gently brushing back a strand of wet hair that had been plastered there. "Sometimes it feels like the crowd is waiting for somebody to get creamed. Screaming for it. They're bloodthirsty, like at a bullfight, especially when they sense a weakness."

"I never felt that way."

"No, I don't imagine you would."

She wanted to move. She couldn't. She was mesmerized by the intensity of his gaze, the shape of his lips, the tiny scar near his right eyebrow that she hadn't noticed before. The slight bump on the bridge of his nose that suggested it had been broken, perhaps more than once.

Everything about Garrett spoke of masculinity and power, determination to play even when in pain, yet underlying it all was a tenderness she wasn't sure he even knew existed. A tenderness that drew her like a feeding bin drew a hungry pig. Except, unlike the animals she raised, Charity might well overindulge herself in the sweet taste of temptation. She had succumbed years ago. Based on her feelings now, there was no reason to suspect she'd learned her lesson.

That would be the height of foolishness.

He touched her again, his fingertips blazing a path

across her lips. "I'm going to have to leave, cinnamon girl."

No! Dear heaven, in spite of every vow she'd ever made to herself, Charity didn't want him to go. "You can't. You don't have a car. Bud did something to mine—"

"The tractor's working. Bud left the key in it. I won't chew up too much asphalt driving it into town."

The sense of imminent loss pressed down on her chest so heavily she could hardly breathe. "Can you stay for lunch?" she asked almost desperately.

One side of his lips quirked into a half smile. "Ham salad is my all-time favorite sandwich. I wouldn't miss yours for the world." He lifted himself up to his knees and winced. "Assuming I can still stand, that is."

Chapter Five

It felt like one of the summer hay rides Charity remembered from her childhood.

The old tractor chuffed and clattered along the side of the road heading into town. Of course, this time it wasn't pulling a hay wagon and Gramps wasn't behind the wheel.

Garrett was.

After lunch he'd convinced Charity to come along for the ride so she could have the cuff removed from her ankle. Assuming they could find the key in the sheriff's office.

Donnie was in seventh heaven, sitting in Garrett's lap, *driving* the tractor; Charity was standing next to them holding on for dear life. To any strangers passing by, they surely would have looked like a family on an afternoon outing.

That wasn't the case.

Garrett was going back to his own life. Charity told herself that it was for the best. If he hung around too long, he'd surely do a little mental math and come up with an answer she would have to vehemently deny. If she admitted the truth, she and Bud would lose the farm, her grandfather's dreams and the legacy passed down from the first Arden settler here in the valley.

"Hey, Mom, there's Shaun Ritters." Excited, Donnie waved to his school friend, who was whizzing along the sidewalk on his skateboard being pulled by his big mixed-breed lab.

"Pay attention to the road, son," Garrett said. "We don't want to have an accident, do we?"

Donnie quickly went back to the serious task of keeping the tractor from driving right up onto the sidewalk with Shaun and his dog.

As they lurched along, Charity's heart constricted. Garrett had called Donnie *son.*

THE TOWN SQUARE only had one traffic light, which appeared programmed for maximum red time in all four directions, allowing motorists and pedestrians alike to view the display windows of Harmon's Department Store for as long as possible. Amazingly the tractor chuffed through on the green.

In the heat of the day, the flag hanging from the pole in the center of City Hall Square drooped limply, and only two youngsters were in the park, tossing a ball back and forth with little enthusiasm. The scent of hamburgers and cooking grease that always seemed to emanate from the Good Eats Diner hovered thickly in the air. Razz Fiddle, who had inherited the diner from his mother, must have had a big lunchtime crowd.

The run on antacids at the drugstore would no doubt come later.

In front of city hall, Garrett pulled into a parking slot that was reserved for the mayor.

"You'll get a ticket if you park here," Charity

warned. "Mayor Harmon is pretty fussy about who parks in his spot."

"So if he complains, I'll let Bud pay for the ticket."

Wonderful! Didn't Garrett realize the fine would come out of her household budget, too?

"Besides," he continued, lifting Donnie from his lap, "as far as we know, the sheriff is still off somewhere tracking down those shotgun-toting bad guys. With any luck, she's got her ticket book with her."

"I hardly think that's possible since she was wearing her wedding gown when she left." That was the first wedding in a series of botched photography jobs Charity had counted on to provide a little cushion for her typically tight finances.

Dismounting from the tractor, they headed for the sheriff's office adjacent to city hall. At almost the same moment, three adolescent boys—bulked-up, long-haired football players—came sauntering out of the nearby bakery, each of them munching on an oversize chocolate-chip cookie.

"Hey, Keeley!" the boy in the middle said, spotting Garrett. "How's it goin', man?"

"Yo, man. How's the knee?" the leanest of the bunch asked.

"You gonna get back to the Niners this season?" the third kid asked. "They're sure gonna need you."

Dutifully Garrett gave each youngster a high five. The boys looked like three-quarters of Grazer Unified High School's front line. Clearly they idolized the school's most famous football graduate and probably wanted to emulate his success.

"Don't count me out yet, fellas. I specialize in comebacks, you know."

"Way to go!" the boys chorused.

Garrett gave one of the youngsters a light punch to his paunchy midsection. "You keep eating those cookies, and Coach Riddler will have you doing sit-ups for the whole season. When you're not sitting on the bench."

"Aw, man..." the boy complained.

"I'd start losing some of those extra pounds now, if I were you," Garrett warned. "Before the preseason practices start. Riddler will run your legs off."

"Yeah, yeah. I know." The young man in question looked around trying to find somewhere to ditch his cookie.

"I'll take it," Donnie piped up.

Charity snared her son by his arm. "No, you won't. You'll spoil your dinner."

"Aw, Mom, we just had lunch."

After a couple more high fives, the adolescent jocks wandered off down the sidewalk, without—thankfully—having contributed to a sugar high for Donnie.

"You appear to have a fan club here in town," Charity said to Garrett.

His lips curled into a smile. "Wanna join? I'll let you be president."

With a haughty toss of her hair, she said, "Thanks, but I think I'll pass."

He acknowledged her refusal with an unconcerned shrug, as if he had plenty of fans without her. Which he no doubt did. "Those kids don't know how lucky they are—playing for Coach Riddler, I mean. My years at Grazer High were great."

Charity hadn't really known him then, though she'd been aware of him around town and had admired him from afar. By the time she was in high school, he was a college hero, a role model whose footsteps the boys had all wanted to follow. Evidently, even with Garrett's recent problems, they still did.

"Every couple of years," she said, "those youngsters you're so fond of at Grazer High decide to see how drunk they can get our hogs. I think it's an initiation of some sort. They wait till we're not home, then the boys show up with a case of beer and everybody gets soused, human and hogs alike."

"I take it Rambo objects."

"On the contrary. He drinks until he can't stand up straight. Then it takes him a week to get over his hangover. Even if we have some sows in estrus and want them serviced, he can't—"

"Serviced?"

"You know..." Heat flooded Charity's cheeks. "Get them pregnant."

"The poor guy!" Garrett burst out laughing. "I've never in my life been that drunk!"

With a simple twist of the knob, she opened the door to the sheriff's office, saving herself the embarrassment of having to continue the conversation. Why had she even brought up the subject? Sometimes she forgot city dwellers didn't discuss the mating habits of farm animals as casually as a breeder did.

Not that she should have brought up the topic of sex—or getting pregnant—with Garrett at all.

"Just like the old days—unlocked doors have gotta say something about the crime rate here in Grazer's Corners," Garrett said, shaking his head as they went inside. "Apparently nobody's worried about vandals."

"I guess with no sheriff in town, Jeanie decided to take a vacation. Not that her dispatching job ever kept her very busy."

The office smelled slightly musty. The reception desk was strewed with unopened mail, and there were Wanted posters piled on one corner of the desk.

Garrett marched straight to a ring of keys hanging on the wall next to the single jail cell the town pointed to with pride as its symbol of legal justice. The most the cell had ever confined was a drunk or two—human, not four-legged. Now the barred door stood open.

"Sit down over there." Garrett gestured toward a straight-back chair, one used for interrogations, Charity suspected. "Let me see if I can find a key that works."

Curious, Donnie wandered into the cell. "If I did somethin' really, really bad, would you lock me up in here, Mom."

"No, dear, I'd make you clean out the pig parlor every day for a year."

"Oh, yuck."

She laughed and sat where Garrett had instructed. A moment later, he knelt in front of her, palming her calf to lift her leg. The heat of his hand warmed her skin through the denim jeans she wore as easily as if she'd been wearing nothing at all.

He had particularly large hands with long, tapered fingers, the key to his ability to effortlessly sail a football almost the length of the field. That, combined with innate talent and hard work, had made him so successful, she supposed. He was used to aggression, slamming his way through a line of players determined to tackle him. Yet he could be incredibly gentle, too.

As he juggled the keys, trying to find one to fit the shackle, she remembered how tenderly he had held her after they had made love all those years ago, how he had caressed her. She'd known at the time it had been a mistake to give herself to Garrett. But she couldn't entirely regret it. Even now.

"Somebody ought to get this place organized," he muttered in frustration, trying yet another key.

Studying the top of his bent head, Charity marveled at the variegated shades of gold and brown, and the effect of cowlicks that made his hair look slightly rumpled even after he'd combed it. She wanted to smooth the waves into place but knew it would be a futile gesture. Like her own hair, Garrett's had a mind of its own.

Little wonder Donnie had curly hair, too. He'd gotten a double dose of that particular gene.

The shackle clicked open. He rubbed her ankle, sending an unexpected wave of pleasure up her leg, and her insides clenched.

"Free at last," Garrett said. "What a relief, huh?" He sat back on his haunches to unlock the shackle on his own ankle.

No, she wasn't free. But Garrett was. He'd go on with his life much as he had before.

He tossed the shackles on the desk, and they rounded up Donnie. It wasn't until they were on the tractor that Charity realized he wasn't taking them back to the farm.

"You can't drive this tractor down residential

streets,'' she warned. ''The whole city council will get after you, not just the mayor.''

Old Victorian houses lined the street, the nicest neighborhood in town with large lots and neatly kept yards. Overhanging trees formed a canopy above the street, providing a deep, cooling shade in the summer. Some of the wealthiest people in town lived here, those who made their living by owning or managing local businesses rather than depending upon farm or vineyard income for their livelihoods. The place reeked of old money and a status Charity had never dreamed of achieving.

The tractor chuffed to a stop in front of the largest house on the block, one that had been meticulously restored a few years ago and Charity had always secretly coveted.

A prickle of suspicion skated down her spine.

''Don't tell me this is your house,'' she said.

Garrett handed Donnie down to her. ''Okay, I won't.''

''Wow, Mom, it looks like somethin' from a movie.'' Donnie raced to the wrought-iron fence that ran across the front of the spacious yard and peered inside like a poor little waif from the country. Which he was.

''This place really belongs to you, Garrett?''

''It does indeed. It was Hailey's idea that we should have a house here in town.''

''She has wonderful taste,'' Charity admitted, simultaneously tamping down a stab of envy and wondering how well Hailey would adjust to living on a pig farm. ''Of all the houses on the block, this has always been my favorite. You were lucky it was on the market.''

"Yeah, right. Now I'll probably have to sell it and take a loss. It's a little big for a bachelor."

"What a shame." She gazed at the house wistfully. "It might not come on the market again for twenty or thirty years." Though it was unlikely she'd have the money to buy it then, either. Not that she'd ever want to leave the farm. But having a house this nice was a whole different matter.

And then it struck her that Garrett had really intended to live here with his bride—a bride who'd run off with Charity's brother.

"I'm so sorry, Garrett. All your plans... You must be heartbroken about losing Hailey."

He leaned back against the front tractor wheel, looking incongruous in Bud's shirt and his own tuxedo pants as he gazed toward the house. "Strangely, no. Maybe our parents pushed too hard, and we both gave in too easily. We went along with what everybody expected us to do." He shoved away from the tractor and headed toward the walkway. "Or maybe I'm not capable of love at all, and she was smart enough to figure that out before it was too late."

A band squeezed tight around Charity's heart at his admission. What a terrible thing for a man to think about himself. Of course Garrett was capable of love.

A long time ago, Charity had seen the depth of Garrett's compassion. She'd been in junior high school, awkward and gangly, the victim of taunts from children who thought a "pig farmer" was something dirty. Usually their words didn't hurt her, but on that particular day they'd been so cruel, she'd been brought to tears.

Passing by, Garrett had intervened. He'd shown a

kindness that surpassed most of the men she'd known since, a kind of love for the underdog that spoke volumes about what was in a man's heart.

She suspected it was at that precise moment she had first fallen in love with Garrett Keeley. And doubted he would even remember the incident.

"Come on, you two," Garrett called. "I'll give you the grand tour and then take you home. In my *car.* Bud can come get the tractor whenever he's so inclined."

She ought to turn down his invitation, get on the tractor and head for home. She was perfectly capable of driving the tractor herself. But her curiosity got the better of her. A few minutes in the house she'd admired for so many years could hardly matter. It wouldn't hurt to look inside.

It was all she had imagined, and less.

The stairway to the second floor curved as beautifully as any sculpture she'd ever seen; the mahogany banister gleamed. The hardwood floors shone with a high gloss. But the downstairs rooms were mostly empty with only scattered pieces of furniture and musty-looking books with titles like *The Revolutionary War in Perspective* stashed in one corner.

"I was going to leave the decorating up to Hailey," Garrett explained. "Guess she found something else to do with her time."

Charity chuckled wryly. "I know I'm just his sister, but it's hard to believe Bud has that much appeal. I'd give my eyeteeth to furnish a house like this." She strolled across the living room, mentally positioning couches and wing-back chairs near the fireplace, placing a filigreed secretary desk near the windows that looked outside, bookcases on the opposite wall. It would cost a fortune to furnish—

"The old couple I bought the house from moved into an upscale retirement home in Modesto. They took some of the furniture with them, and some of the really nice pieces they gave to their kids. Fortunately most of the bedrooms are still habitable."

The *bedrooms.* She glanced up the stairs. Yes, with Garrett, having the bedrooms furnished would be important—and something Charity shouldn't be thinking about. And her heart shouldn't have stuttered at the mere mention of the word. Sophisticated, she wasn't.

Donnie, who'd gone wandering off on his own, came thundering into the room, his shoes like bullets on the hardwood floors.

"Mom, ya gotta come see! Garrett's got a whole mess of exercise stuff. Barbells and bicycles and stuff. There's even a swimmin' pool. Come see!"

She raised her eyebrows. "An indoor pool?"

"Not quite. A Jacuzzi. Old jocks need all the help they can get with their sore muscles."

"You're not so old." About twenty-nine or thirty, she thought, four years her senior.

"My knees are," he said wryly. "According to the NFL doctors, at any rate."

She realized he hated losing his job as a quarterback but she didn't know what to say. The fact was, she'd just as soon he was never sacked again. To watch him go down under a thousand pounds of charging linemen hurt *her* too much.

They toured the downstairs, including an exercise room and a kitchen that was as modern as any a gourmet chef would dream about, and then they went upstairs. Their voices echoed in the hallway.

"You have enough room here to house an army," Charity commented. "Hailey must have been planning on a big family."

"We never talked about kids."

Her head snapped up, and she came to an abrupt halt. "Don't you want children?"

"I don't know. I don't think I'd be all that good a dad."

"How can you say that? You're wonderful with Donnie."

"That's in the short haul. For the long term, I'm not sure I had a real good role model."

"But you love your father."

"I feel an obligation to my dad, a sense of duty. But I was never quite able to live up to his expectations. I wouldn't want a son of my own to feel that way."

"I guess you'll have to break the news to your parents that you didn't elope after all."

"I'm not looking forward to it."

Unable to resist, she reached out to him. They were standing in the hallway, facing each other, and her hand rested on his chest, his heart beating beneath her palm. So solid. So strong. That he would doubt himself for even a moment tore at Charity's heart and constricted her throat.

"You would be the most wonderful father in the world," she whispered. *And lover, too.*

"You'd think that, cinnamon girl." His voice husky, he covered her hand with his. "Nice to have somebody on my side."

"Always."

Her heart beat harder. She could barely draw a breath. The air crackled with electricity as though a storm were about to hit. The green in his eyes nearly vanished into a dark pool of black. Charity wavered, her knees weak, and she leaned toward him.

"Mom! You gotta see this bed! It's *huuuge!*"

Charity jumped back like she'd been shot. This was *not* a good time to be thinking about beds—particularly Garrett's. The bed he'd intended to share with his bride.

"I think we'd better be going," she said. She pulled her braid around to the front of her shoulder, fiddling nervously with loose strands.

He studied her a moment before he said, "I'll get my car keys."

"No! I, ah, might need the tractor before Bud gets home. And my car is still out of whack," she reminded him. "Thanks to my thoughtful brother."

His forehead pleated. "You sure you can drive it okay?"

"I've been doing it since I was Donnie's age, Garrett. That's what farm kids do."

As though he was unwilling to let her go and wanted to keep her talking, he asked, "How old is Donnie?"

She backed up another step, more intent on escape than his question. Her palm was still tingling with the heat of his body; she had to get away. She had to stop wanting things that couldn't be. "He turned seven in May. They grow up so fast, it's hard to believe he'll be in second grade this fall."

"I imagine that's true."

"Donnie!" she called. "Time to go, honey."

"Aw, Mom..." He appeared at the doorway to the master bedroom. "Can't we—?"

"No, we can't."

He jammed his hands into his jeans pockets, then looked up hopefully at Garrett. "If you come visit again, I'll show you where some ducks lay their eggs. There's always broken shells and stuff from the foxes eatin' 'em."

Hooking his hand around the boy's neck, Garrett smiled. "Sounds like a chance I couldn't pass up. If your mom wouldn't mind me dropping by sometime."

"Of course not," she said quickly. Too quickly. Her son was so taken with Garrett, she was afraid of what might happen if Garrett didn't keep his promise. Or if he did, and realized it was his own son he was visiting.

Garrett went downstairs with Charity and the boy and walked with them out to the tractor. The street was quiet; no kids were playing in the staid, well-kept yards. No one had organized a street baseball game or chalked off yard markers for football. Probably finding broken duck eggs would be more fun for a kid than living here.

He watched as she climbed into the driver's seat and settled Donnie in front of her.

"If the highway patrol gives me a ticket," she said, teasing, "I'll tell them to forward it to Grazer High's most famous alum."

"Sounds fair enough to me. Didn't we have some grad who got sent to jail for murdering—?"

"Oh, you..." Waving him off, she laughed. The sound was as musical as the birds in the trees that lined the street, as warm and welcoming as hot chocolate on a cold winter night.

As the tractor chugged down the street, Garrett decided Charity was probably the most competent woman he'd ever met. In contrast to Hailey, she never would have let her family talk her—however temporarily—into marrying a man she didn't love. She would have fought it tooth and nail.

Granted, she might not be as classically beautiful as Hailey—or as most of the women he'd dated. But at her core she was one hell of a woman.

Heading back into the house—so empty it echoed with lost promises—he tried to remember precisely how long ago it had been when he and Charity had made love at the lake. It was late summer, he thought, because he'd gone back to the university shortly after that. But exactly what year had that been?

The phone rang as he entered the house, disrupting his thoughts.

He picked up the instrument.

''Hey, Keeley, my man,'' the caller said, his voice so booming Garrett immediately knew it was his agent, Tommy Lubcheck, former Pro Bowl Viking linebacker. ''You musta gotten back early from your honeymoon, huh?''

''Not exactly,'' Garret hedged, holding the phone a couple of inches away from his ear. ''What's up?''

''Nothing good, I'm afraid. Was just gonna leave a message on your machine.''

''Go ahead. I'll pretend I'm not here.''

''Yeah, well, it's the Saints. They considered bringing you on board as a backup quarterback, but folded at the last minute. They picked up Terry Westin from Northwestern instead.''

''He's a rookie, for God's sake. And he didn't have all that good a year.'' *But he has two good knees.* The truth of those words, and their import, reverberated through Garrett's mind. If he couldn't rehabilitate his knee—

''I know. I know. Don't worry. I'm talkin' to a couple of other teams about you. The preseason's always hard on quarterbacks. Injuries, you know. And some of 'em just can't hack it. I'm not giving up on you, man.''

His fingers tightened in near desperation around the phone. ''I appreciate that, Tommy.''

''Well, kiss the bride for me. I'll be in touch.''

''Thanks, Tommy. Talk to you later.''

Garrett cradled the phone. With a snarl of frustration, he splayed his fingers through his hair. He had more talent in one hand than that kid from Northwestern... Not that it mattered to the boys who held the purse strings.

Sighing, he went in search of a beer in the kitchen.

It was quiet in the house with him all alone. If he couldn't sell the place, he'd have to rent out rooms.

His lips quirked. Too bad Charity and her son were so happy living on that subsistence farm of hers. He'd invite them to come stay with him.

But he'd draw the line at inviting Rambo.

He popped the tab on the can.

Procrastination wasn't going to work forever. His folks would be wondering what the hell had happened to him.

He wasn't exactly thrilled at the prospect of explaining to his father that he had failed again.

There was something else bothering him, too. Something Charity had said.

Chapter Six

She heard Bud's truck in the driveway just as she was serving Donnie his dinner. Hailey's Cherokee pulled in right behind him.

It had been an impossibly long day—after an equally interminable night. Garrett's presence still hovered in the house—the faint trace of his masculine scent; Charity's far more potent memories; the indentation of his head on the pillow next to hers, which, perversely, she had been unwilling to fluff back into shape.

In spite of some residual anger still directed at Bud for his shenanigans, she was relieved to have her brother and his bride back home. At least they'd fill the house with new sounds, new scents. The memories of Garrett would linger in her mind, however, as they had so powerfully for the past eight years.

The truck door slammed.

"Is that Garrett? He said he'd come." Donnie popped up from the kitchen table ready to race outside.

"It's your uncle Bud."

"Oh." His enthusiasm waned.

"And your aunt Hailey," Charity reminded him.

This time he pulled a face.

"Remember your manners, young man. Hailey's a part of our family now. An Arden just like you and me." Founders of Grazer's Corners, whether acknowledged or not. Immigrants from the east at the turn of the century who'd struggled and survived. Their memories deserved to be honored.

His shoulders slumped. "Yeah, I guess. Garrett said I was supposed to give her a chance. He said she's pretty."

"Yes, well..." Her throat tightened. Hailey was far more Garrett's type than she was, model thin with classic features and glossy blond hair. Not a woman whose hair frizzed even on desert-dry days. "Hailey's very attractive."

The screen door at the front of the house creaked open.

"Sis, we're home. Anybody here?"

Cupping the back of Donnie's head, Charity ushered him into the living room to greet his new aunt, determined the young woman would feel welcomed into the family. She forcefully tamped down questions she had about Hailey's relationship with Garrett and the accompanying flare of unwanted jealousy. "We're here," she called.

Bud stepped gingerly into the room. He glanced around, then focused on his sister and frowned. "Where's Garrett?"

"Gone."

"But you were supposed to—"

"I don't think Garrett liked your practical joke, Uncle Bud. He and Mom couldn't do nothin' without each other."

"How'd he get loose?"

"I found the bolt cutters in the toolshed." She shook her head at her brother. "You'd sure better have that gizmo you took out of my car. I want it all put back—"

"I'll fix it later. Has he called the cops on us?" Bud asked, a trace of panic in his voice.

"No. But you're lucky he didn't. This was a fool stunt you pulled, Bud. I ought to throttle you myself." That was an empty threat since her brother stood about six inches taller than Charity and outweighed her by a hundred pounds. *Big brother* in Bud's case was an understatement. That didn't prevent Charity from being mad at him, however.

"I thought maybe you and Garrett would...I don't know. Chained together like you were..."

"Bud, you stole his bride. What the devil did you think he and I would—?"

From behind Bud, Hailey appeared. She smiled sheepishly. "Guess we really put you in an awkward spot, didn't we?"

More awkward than you'll ever know, she thought. Extending her arms, she crossed the room to the woman who had very likely been Garrett's lover, an image she quickly set aside. "Welcome to the family, Hailey. May you and Bud have many years of happiness together."

Hailey's blue eyes sheened with tears as she accepted Charity's embrace. "Thank you. I'm so sorry for whatever trouble we caused you. I just couldn't go through with my marriage to Garrett, not when I've always loved Bud so much. And it's not like Garrett doesn't have dozens of other women who'd be more than happy to marry him."

Stepping back, Charity was torn by her feelings for Garrett and not wanting to offend her new sister-in-law. She opted for diplomacy. "I suppose that's true. But he was hurt, Hailey. There had to be some other—"

"I'll bet he's already got some girl shacking up with him," Bud said, looping his arm around Hailey's shoulders and pulling her close. "He probably never stopped seeing other women, even when he and Hailey were planning to get married."

Shocked, Charity said, "I don't think he's like that." He'd said that he'd loved Hailey, or thought he had. He wouldn't have been two-timing her.

"Hell, Garrett's always had more women than you could shake a stick at," Bud said. "You shoulda heard the locker-room talk when he was in high school. He made out anytime he crooked his little finger."

Charity had heard the rumors, but she'd assumed if he were engaged he would be faithful. The thought that he might not have been made her slightly sick to her stomach.

"Well, it doesn't matter now, does it, Buddy," Hailey crooned. She lifted her face to her groom and he kissed her, all too deeply.

Charity wanted to cover Donnie's eyes. "I didn't know when to expect you two. Have you had dinner yet?"

It took them a while to come up for air.

Donnie made a hasty exit, mumbling, "Yuck, I hate mushy stuff."

Charity was about to follow her son out of the room when Bud said, "We stopped for burgers, thanks, anyway." He planted another solid kiss on

Hailey's lips. "It's been a long ride back from Vegas. Think I'll show my bride her new bedroom. We'll tell you all about the wedding later." Hardly glancing in Charity's direction, he escorted Hailey down the hallway. It looked like they might be occupied for a long time.

The childish expression "Gag me with a spoon" popped into her head. It was going to be very different having two lovebirds living in the house. She'd have to remind Bud to knock it off with blatant displays of affection in front of Donnie. *And* herself.

With considerable effort, she quashed a rising sense of envy that her brother had found someone to love while she had not. He deserved whatever happiness he could find, and so did Hailey. Bud had given up a promising future as an engineer when he'd dropped out of college to work the farm. And through all these years, never once had he pressed to know who had fathered Donnie. He'd simply been there for her when she needed a big brother to rely on.

Because of that, she tried not to think about what he had said about Garrett. Though not friends, Bud and Garrett had attended high school at the same time. Her brother had probably heard a lot of things, most of them true, she suspected. But that had been a long time ago. She didn't want to believe now that Garrett couldn't be faithful to a woman.

But perhaps it was true.

Maybe I'm not capable of love he had told her. Or of being faithful to a woman? she wondered. What would a man like that be as a father to her son? Not the role model she'd prefer.

In spite of the warm day, she shivered. She'd never be able to endure infidelity. If Hailey had suspected Garrett of that, little wonder she chose Bud instead.

SHE'D JUST FINISHED washing up the dinner dishes and was drying her hands when she heard another car in the driveway. Their farm had become a regular Grand Central Station, she thought with a sigh.

"Hey, Mom!" Donnie yelled from the living room. "It's Garrett!" An instant later, the screen door slammed and Donnie's footsteps pounded across the front porch.

Charity's insides clenched, and her heart rate accelerated.

Dear Lord, less than an hour ago she'd been told Garrett wasn't a man capable of fidelity. And still she reacted that way to the news of his arrival. She didn't have the sense God gave a hog. At least Rambo, given a choice, preferred monogamous relationships with his lady loves. For as long as they were in estrus, anyway.

Tossing the towel aside, she called down the hallway to her brother. "You'd better come out, Bud. I suspect Garrett's here to talk with you." And she hoped he hadn't brought a gun with him.

When she reached the porch, Garrett was hunkered down at eye level with Donnie and engaged in a deep conversation. He'd discarded the tuxedo pants he'd worn earlier, replacing them with faded jeans that gloved his tight butt with the softness of a woman's hand. Something about the way he was clasping the boy's shoulder and looking intently into his eyes made her breath catch. It was the way a father might talk to his son.

No! He couldn't know, not for sure. Even if he'd begun speculating about the dates, that's all it could be. Speculation. Guesswork. A little curiosity.

Drawing a deep breath, she walked to her son's side, resisting the urge to draw him to her. "Bud will be out in a minute," she told Garrett.

He looked up at her, his brows pulled together. In his eyes, she saw questions that she'd never be able, or willing, to answer. Conjectures, that's all he had.

"Actually I wanted to talk to Hailey," he said, standing. His eyes were on Charity, penetrating like deep green stilettos. "Her folks are going out of their heads with worry."

"She should have stopped by to see them first thing when they got back. Or at least called."

He nodded his agreement. "Then later, after I talk to her, I think you and I need to have a little chat."

Her throat seized. She managed a nonchalant shrug and a croaky "Sure."

"Garrett says maybe later he can come see the broken duck eggs, Mom. Is that okay?"

As though his gaze were a powerful magnet fed by an electric current, she couldn't look away. "Of course, honey. Just try not to get your shoes too muddy." Blindly she reached out to her son. Wanting to hold him to her and never let go. But he was gone.

She gasped and looked around. He'd scampered off to the old tire swing hanging from an oak tree in the front yard. He clambered into it, set on showing off to his new idol.

His father.

The truth twisted in her like a tightly coiled spring pulling taut.

"Watch me!" he shouted, pumping the swing hard.

But the arrival of Bud and his bride on the front porch distracted Garrett. He riveted his attention on the woman he had planned to marry three days ago. From the look of her, he'd guess she'd just had sex. Good sex. Her cheeks were flushed, her usually carefully styled hair in slight disarray. Oddly enough, the sight of her like that didn't bother him as much as it should. He ought to be in a rage, jealous as hell. But he simply didn't care.

Not that he wasn't miffed she'd picked another man over him.

"You need to call your folks," he said. "They're worried sick."

Hailey's eyes widened. "You talked with them?"

"They had to hear the story from someone. You weren't around."

She went a little pale, and Garrett might have felt sorry for her except she was in a mess of her own making. "It would have been easier if you'd told me you didn't want to get married," he said. That might have let him admit he didn't want to go through with the ceremony, either. "Together we could have convinced your folks it wasn't right for either of us."

"I'm sorry," she whispered.

Bud's protective arm around Hailey's shoulder tightened ever so slightly. "We'll go see the Olsons now. Given enough time, they'll accept that she's chosen me."

"I'm sure that's true." Not that Hailey's parents would have much choice. What's done was done. They'd all have to live with it. "Good luck."

"Look, Garrett, I don't want there to be any hard feelings over this," Bud said. "I mean, you'll have lots of chances—"

"Don't press your luck, Bud. It's only because Charity doesn't like violence that I haven't pounded you into the ground, just on general principles."

Bud shot Garrett a look, then gave Charity a sideways glance, finally lifting his shoulders in a shrug.

As the bridal couple turned to go inside, Garrett caught Charity's arm. She was wearing a tank top and jeans, and her skin was as soft as warm velvet. "Let's go find someplace to talk. Alone."

NAUSEA BURNED in Charity's throat. The tacos she'd had for dinner—Donnie's favorite—were about to rebel. She had to go with Garrett. Had to act as though nothing was wrong. Had to *bluff,* if need be. The very existence of the Arden farm depended upon it.

He walked them around toward the back of the house. The row of sunflowers she'd planted along the walkway lifted their heads toward the summer sun, which was still well above the horizon although it was close to seven o'clock. Sparrows and starlings darted through the air, snatching up insects. From the pond, the frogs were beginning an evening's discussion; the pigs in the parlor were chattering contentedly.

When they went through the gate to the farmyard, Rambo trotted over to her and nuzzled her hand.

"Sorry, fella," she apologized. "No nibblies tonight."

He nudged her again, a thousand pounds on the hoof. She tried to step away, but Garrett was right there.

Their hips collided; their arms brushed. His heat whipped through her, curling into her midsection. She wanted to be somewhere else; she wanted to be with him.

"I've been doing some thinking," Garrett began. "Some calculating, actually."

Somewhere else.

Rambo woofed a sound of piglike warning and angled himself across the path, forcing Charity to take the fork to the pig parlor.

Caught between Garrett and the hog, she nearly stumbled. "Rambo, what are you doing?"

"I'm trying to talk to you, Charity. About Donnie. How 'bout telling your overweight bodyguard to get lost?"

Rambo got behind her, bumping her rear end with his snout.

She hop-skipped ahead. "Rambo, cut that out!" Didn't she have enough to worry about without being goosed by an overzealous Yorkshire hog who thought he was a guard dog?

"That night at the lake," Garrett continued. "The night we—"

Rambo bumped her again, and she whirled. "What on earth is the matter with you?"

Oooonnneeekk! Insistent. Determined.

"Oh, my gosh," she gasped. "There's something wrong."

She broke into a run. Behind her, she heard

Rambo galloping after her, followed by Garrett's footsteps on the path.

"What is it?" Garrett shouted, trying to keep up with Charity. She was as agile and quick as a receiver on a long passing route to the goal line. Wherever the hell that might be on a pig farm.

She raced into the pig parlor and made a beeline for the pen where Garrett had seen the pregnant sow. She knelt beside the shuddering animal just as a piglet, all slippery and wet, slid out of its mother.

Looking up at Garrett, breathing hard, Charity said, "It's Sweet Pea." She soothed the animal's head as she spoke. "She wasn't due to deliver for a couple of days yet. I guess Rambo thought I ought to be here in case anything went wrong."

The damn hog knew? "Is she okay?"

"I think so."

As she said the words, the sow oinked and out plopped another slippery little creature, its ears pulled back, its umbilical cord still tethering it to its mother. In a fascinating rhythm of grunt, oink and plop, another two babies arrived. They groped blindly through the bedding straw for their mother's teats and latched on.

Charity continued to stroke the sow's head, murmuring soft words of encouragement. "She's beautiful, isn't she?"

Oddly enough, the sow did look... Well, Garrett wouldn't describe her as beautiful. Content, perhaps. And more so with each little creature that popped out of her distended belly.

What was truly beautiful was the ethereal look of joy on Charity's face. She was seeing the moment of birth as only another mother could, each offspring perfect, each worthy of her devotion. Oddly it struck him as awe-inspiring that a big lummox like Rambo and Sweet Pea could create such perfect little replicas of themselves.

A lump tightened in Garrett's throat as he wondered if he and Charity had done the same in one careless, passionate evening of making love. Could they have created something even more stunning? A child? Donnie?

If they had, he should have been there with her at the moment of birth. It was too extraordinary an event to miss.

With the ease of experience, Charity picked up each piglet in turn—there were eight in all now—and whispered what sounded like a welcome as she tied off its umbilical cord. She worked a moment more on each little creature before returning it to its mother's side.

When she looked at Garrett, she glowed with pride. His heart nearly seized.

"Charity..." Emotion thickened in his throat, making him hoarse. He forced himself to say the words. "Is Donnie my son?"

She paled and glanced away. Her fingers trembled as she placed the last of the piglets back in the pen. "Why would you ask a strange question like that?" Her voice lacked any trace of emotion. An automaton's response. And phony as hell.

A muscle pumped at Garrett's jaw. She was lying. But why? Why would a woman lie about who had fathered her child?

"We made love, Charity. Or don't you remember?" His jaw ached from clenching it so hard waiting for her answer.

She stood, and an irritating little shrug lifted her shoulders. "Of course I remember. That doesn't mean you got me pregnant. You used a condom, didn't you?"

Had he? Dammit, he couldn't remember. It had been so long ago. But he'd always been careful. He'd never wanted any accidents, any encumbrances. Having kids had never been part of his agenda. "Condoms aren't foolproof," he reminded her.

"Don't worry about it, Garrett. If I'd been eager to nail you with a paternity suit, I would have done it a long time ago."

"I'm not talking about suing anybody. I want to know the truth."

Eyes never meeting his, she walked out of the pig parlor with her spine ramrod straight. "You're not Donnie's father."

He followed her. He could feel her lies; they washed over him like an acid bath. "The timing was right."

"You don't know that."

"I can count."

"Well, count again," she said, turning. "You're not the only man in the world, Garrett Keeley. You never have been."

A jealous rage thrummed through him. Another man? He didn't want to believe it. He wouldn't believe it. "What if I demanded a blood test?"

"I wouldn't permit it. That's invasion of privacy, and you'd need my permission to so much as prick Donnie's little finger."

"I could get a court order."

"On what basis? Because you *think* he might be

your son? He doesn't exactly resemble you, does he? He doesn't have some unique birthmark that only appears on a long line of Keeley males. Get real! There's nothing to say you are in any way related to him."

"So who is his father?"

"That is none of your business."

They stood glaring at each other, the long rays of the setting sun touching Charity's hair like a halo and catching in her eyes with glistening, red-gold shards of determination that flashed back at him. He'd never known a woman more stubborn—or one who lied with such beautiful insistence. But why? he kept wondering.

If he wasn't the father, what dark secret was she hiding that she wouldn't reveal even a hint of who the man might be?

"Hey, Garrett!" Donnie called from across the way near the pond. "Aren't ya gonna come see? It's gonna be dark soon."

She glanced over her shoulder and back to Garrett again, her eyes both imploring and demanding. "If you so much as breathe a word of this harebrained idea of yours to my son, I'll be the one doing the suing, and it won't be about paternity. It'll be about defamation of character."

"Maybe if you sued, I'd learn the truth."

"I've told you the only truth you need to know. You are *not* Donnie's father."

CHARITY BARELY MADE IT into the house before her legs gave way and she sank to the kitchen floor, covering her mouth with her hand to stifle a sob.

She couldn't tell Garrett the truth. Yet lying to

him had been the most difficult, painful thing she'd ever done in her life. Guiltily she knew he had the right to know he had a son. But Douglas Keeley, Garrett's father, had stolen that right. To protect the Arden farm, to retain the home her grandparents had loved and labored for as they slipped toward their final rest and to provide a home for her unborn child, Charity had agreed to Douglas Keeley's terms.

He'd arranged it so there would be no turning back. No revealing the truth. Ever.

Not if she wanted to retain the farm. For herself. For Bud and his bride. For her son.

The strangled sob rose to her throat. Tears filled her eyes. However much she might want it otherwise, she would never be able to acknowledge Garrett as Donnie's father.

THE NEXT MORNING Garrett went in search of Agatha Flintstone, owner of the Book Nook, part-time town clerk and inveterate busybody. What she didn't know about the residents of Grazer's Corners wasn't worth repeating.

He stood on the sidewalk of the town square wondering if she'd be at her store or the city hall. Since the posted hours at both places bore little resemblance to her actual schedule, he had about a fifty-fifty chance of guessing right—or wrong.

What he was after would be in the town's records, so he decided to try city hall first. Angling in that direction, he caught the scent of fresh-baked bread from the bakery and his mouth watered. He hadn't eaten any breakfast; there wasn't much in the house *to* eat. He'd have to correct that oversight later, but now he wanted some answers.

The city hall was laid out like an early California mission with a landscaped courtyard surrounded by offices and a requisite bubbling fountain in the middle. He found the city clerk's office. To his amazement, it was open and Agatha was at her desk. As she sometimes did, she was reading aloud from a paperback book.

"'Her heart pounded, and the flesh of her breasts flamed from his touch,'" Agatha read dramatically. "'No other man had caressed her so, had made her lose all reason with a single kiss. "Gunther," she sobbed...'"

"Excuse me," Garrett interrupted.

Agatha's book flew out of her hand. "Mercy, you gave me a fright."

"I'm sorry, ma'am."

Blinking, she appeared to leave her romantic images in the world of make-believe and rejoin those who were confined by the realities of Grazer's Corners.

"What a terrible thing happened to you, dear boy," she said with as much flair as she'd read her book. "Your bride going off with another man. Not that I don't like Bud, you understand, but you're such a good catch. Makes a body wonder what got into Hailey's head, doesn't it? You'd think there was an epidemic going on in town, what with that sweet Jordan girl going off with a strange man. And Kate before her. Why, I was just reading the most wonderful story about the Normans. They did a lot of kidnapping—"

"Agatha, do you keep the birth records here?"

Her eyes widened. "Is Hailey pregnant?"

"Not that I know of." Though these days, the

most Garrett could be sure of was that Agatha's sources of information rivaled those of the CIA and were a hell of a lot quicker if not always accurate. "I wanted to check through the records for about seven years ago."

"Seven years ago?"

Garrett could almost see the wheels spinning in her retentive little mind, clicking off names and dates with as much speed as her computer would manage. "They're public record, aren't they?"

"Well, yes, but I can't imagine—"

"If you'll just show me where they are, Agatha."

Her lips moved, but no sound came out as she stood and went to a file cabinet at the back of the office. "Now, you can't take any of this with you, you know. And I'm the only one who can make official copies."

"I understand."

With a final, curious look, she opened a big, heavy drawer.

"Thank you, Agatha. I can manage from here." Using his greater height and weight, he edged her aside. He didn't want her to know which specific record he was checking, and certainly not why.

He thumbed through the files until he came to the May births seven years ago. In a town the size of Grazer's Corners, there weren't all that many. He found the one he was looking for easily enough.

In a quick glance, he found the entry he needed but not the answer he wanted: "Father unknown."

Unknown? How the hell could that be? Charity wasn't promiscuous. In fact, though she hadn't said so, he'd suspected she'd been a virgin until that night they'd made love. He'd been so damn proud that he'd been her first lover, and so careful to make sure she enjoyed the experience fully as much as he had.

So what happened? In the next couple of weeks, had she gone to bed with so many guys she couldn't guess which one had gotten her pregnant?

That didn't make any sense. She'd never been that kind of girl.

He shoved the record back into the file folder and slammed the drawer shut. Something screwy was going on here, and he was going to get to the bottom of it. He might not be the best candidate for father of the year, but he'd never been known to shirk his responsibilities.

Chapter Seven

Garrett rounded a corner in the grocery store aisle, and another cart slammed into his wobbly-wheeled one, shoving it into a shelf full of cat food.

"Well!" Charity huffed. "I hope you're satisfied."

Suppressing a smile at the sheer pleasure of seeing her, he cocked his head. "I think you were the one who was going too fast here."

"I don't mean this." She waved vaguely at the cans rolling around on the floor. "I got a call from the high-school principal this morning. From now on, I'm going to have to *bid* to do the pictures for the school annual. That's the steadiest source of income I have."

He did a double take. She was obviously mad as hell. But why at him? "What's that got to do with me?"

"Your father is on the school board, in case you've forgotten. That's what it has to do with you. And there isn't a chance in Hades that I'll get the contract if he has anything to say about it."

"Now, wait a minute—"

"No, you wait." She tried to shove her cart out

of the way but got hung up on a can of chopped liver and chicken. "Your father's also trying to get Bud fired from his job at the factory. He's furious Hailey decided to marry somebody other than his high-and-mighty football-hero son. So he's going to get even any way he can."

Garrett couldn't believe his father would stoop that low. Or maybe he could believe it, but he didn't want to. "It still doesn't have anything to do with me."

She yanked her cart to the side like she was training for a bulldogging event. "If you'll excuse me, I've got shopping to do. I haven't been able to get into town lately. *Houseguests,* you know."

She wheeled around him with the speed and precision of a race car driver, her blue denim skirt swirling around her calves, her sandals flapping angrily on the linoleum floor. He would have laughed except for the crawling feeling inside his gut.

His father had not been pleased with the botched marriage. Being vindictive about the whole thing fit Douglas Keeley's definition of getting even. Garrett would have to check it out.

The fact that he spotted Charity talking to Homer, the butcher, a few minutes later didn't alter Garrett's need to talk with his father. But it sure as hell twisted a knot in his stomach.

Her Saturday date with the man was coming up soon. Garrett didn't even want to think about it.

He completed his shopping, dropped the groceries off at his house and headed for the chocolate factory. His grandfather had founded the Fun House Candy Company north of town because of the proximity to almond, walnut and pistachio groves. In fact there were those who said Grazer's Corners was the nut capital of the world. More than once, Garrett had wondered if they were talking about the almond groves or the residents.

The cloying, bittersweet scent of chocolate struck him in the parking lot as he got out of the car. As much as his family depended on chocolate to produce its income, he'd learned to hate it the one summer his father had made him work on the production line. He'd never wanted to look at, much less eat, a Fruity Tootie Nut Bar since.

The receptionist, a woman in her fifties with blond hair and a surprisingly youthful complexion, preened as he entered the small lobby.

"Hello, Garrett, how are you? I was so sorry to hear about—"

"I'm fine, Arabelle. Is Dad in?"

"I think so. I'd be happy to check for you."

He waved her off. "I'll just go on up. Thanks."

"Well, now, you just let me know if I can help in any way at all. Now that you're a free man again, I mean. *Any* way at all, you hear?" With that provocative invitation, she buzzed him through the security door.

Garrett didn't imagine he'd take her up on the offer. For as long as he could remember, women had been making offers like that, most of which he'd turned down. Not that the tabloids would believe it. Nor did he much care one way or the other.

His father had chosen a second-floor corner office with a view of almond groves in the foreground and the Sierra foothills beyond them. In spring and fall, it was a striking landscape, with the trees either in colorful bloom or covered with golden leaves that contrasted with the snowcapped mountain peaks in the distance.

When Garrett entered the office, Douglas Keeley looked up from the computer printout he'd been studying.

"Hello, son. I didn't know you were going to stop by."

"There are a couple of things I want to talk to you about."

Douglas removed his reading glasses and set them aside. At sixty, he was as tall as Garrett but leaner with hair that only now was shifting from blond to gray. The former UC Berkeley quarterback kept himself fit by working out three times a week, almost as though he was still expecting an NFL team to give him the call that had never come in his youth. The closest he'd come to achieving his dream of a pro-football career he'd accomplished vicariously by having Garrett make it to the big time.

And now Garrett had lost it. Or so everyone thought.

"I hope you've come to tell me you've decided to spend some time learning the candy business," Douglas said.

"I play football, Dad. And my degree's in history. Handling accounts receivable isn't exactly my thing."

"I could use your help, son. I'm not getting any younger, you know. Not that I doubt for a minute some team will pick up your option. You're too damn good for them to overlook you. But eventually you'll need something to fall back on. This is a family business, son."

"I'm still thinking about it, Dad." But not very eagerly. "I wanted to talk to you about the Ardens."

Leaning back in his leather chair, Douglas laced his fingers together and tented them in front of his chin. "The Ardens?"

"Don't play dumb, Dad. You've been making waves."

"I don't know what you're talking about."

"You're trying to undermine Charity's job at Grazer High taking photos for the annual. She depends on that job for her livelihood."

"Now, listen to me, son. All I did was suggest to the school superintendent that contracts like that ought to go out for bids. If she can't be competitive—"

"And if she is?" Garrett planted his hands on his father's desk and leaned closer. "Would she get the job?"

"That would be out of my hands, of course. It's strictly a business decision the superintendent and school board will have to make. And I really don't see how it concerns you."

"It concerns me, okay? If you're mad at Bud Arden for marrying Hailey, don't be. He probably saved me from making a big mistake."

Shoving his chair back, Douglas stood. He'd never liked being backed into a corner. "The Ardens are nothing but trash. Pig farmers, for God's sake. You need to stay as far away from them—both of them—as you can. In fact, if I could, I'd fire Bud in a flash. He's always been a troublemaker."

"Really? Because he helped form the union?" And he was still a union steward, making his job especially secure.

"My employees don't need a union. They never have. Certainly not one Bud Arden has anything to do with."

Garrett had heard differently. Since the union arrived on the scene, paid vacations and a decent retirement plan had been negotiated, benefits the mostly seasonal workers would never have received if they'd waited for management to make the offer.

Idly Garrett picked up the Fun House Candy Company gift catalog from the corner of the desk and thumbed through it, glancing at the photos. He didn't want his father to know just how much he cared about Charity's well-being—and her son's. Douglas could be unpredictable if he thought his will was being thwarted, and he certainly was expressing a lot of animosity toward both of the Ardens. Garrett couldn't help but wonder why. A canceled wedding hardly seemed like sufficient cause for a vendetta.

As he studied the catalog, an idea came to him. An idea that wouldn't exactly please his father.

"Maybe you're right, Dad. Maybe I should get more involved in the company."

His father beamed with pleasure, the biggest smile Garrett had seen in a long while. "Just give the word, son, and I'll have an office arranged for you right next to mine."

"Will I be able to make some management decisions on my own?"

Douglas frowned. "Within limits. I don't want you making any radical changes until you get to know the business."

A smile tugged at Garrett's lips. "You have my word."

CHARITY DIDN'T RECALL *Arsenic and Old Lace* as quite so boring. But perhaps she shouldn't blame either the actors or the playwright. Her restlessness might be due to the man sitting next to her.

Poor Homer! He was doing everything he could to impress her. He'd planned a family dinner with his girls that turned into a disaster—blackened chicken au burned tea towel presented to the accompaniment of the smoke alarm.

Donnie had been at his worst and would get a sound lecture from her in the morning.

Meanwhile Homer was wearing a cologne that was no doubt intended to seduce, but he'd used too much and the fumes wafted around the playhouse in a poisonous release that was probably making everyone within six rows seriously ill. Any moment now, the playhouse management was likely to call a hazardous-materials decontamination team to ventilate the place.

She sighed, and he squeezed her hand in the darkness.

The truth was she wanted to be—anywhere—with Garrett.

Closing her eyes against the glare from the stage, she wondered why she couldn't settle for a perfectly nice man like Homer. She could have his babies. They'd all be a family, albeit a blended family with his, hers and their kids. That wasn't such a terrible thought.

Except that wasn't what she wanted.

Instead of settling for *Arsenic and Old Lace,* she wanted *The Sound of Music.* She wanted heart stopping, soaring passion with a whole lot of romance thrown in. Face it, she wanted Garrett. She always had. Some women never outgrew their adolescent fantasies.

She simply couldn't get him out of her imagination—the sensual shape of his lips, the way his hair curled and waved, wayward locks slipping across his forehead. His taste, which she'd savored all too recently. The tapered length of his fingers. The breadth of his shoulders.

Nothing about Garrett had been lost from her memory, not how he had touched her eight years ago, not how he had looked at her only days ago. She was a conflicted mass of wanting and denial, an emotional and physical mess. If she had any sense at all, she'd bury her head in the sand and block out all the sensations that were butting against her good reason.

But no woman had that much strength. Not when it came to Garrett Keeley.

"That was great, wasn't it?" Homer said as they exited the theater with the rest of the crowd.

"Wonderful," she agreed, grateful for the breath of fresh air when they reached the outdoors.

"Gene Linfield is wasted as a meat cutter," Homer said of his co-worker. "He shoulda been an actor."

"I'm sure his income is a little more secure here in Grazer's Corners than it would be in Hollywood."

"Yeah, I suppose." He slid his arm around her waist. "So how 'bout stopping for ice cream? It's not too late."

"Gee, Homer, I'm awfully tired. Would you mind terribly if I gave you a rain check?" At least she wasn't lying about being tired. She actually felt drained, pressed down with the knowledge that she couldn't *settle* for something less than she wanted deep in her heart. "I think I'd better pick up Donnie and head on home. Sorry to be such a party poop."

"Hey, no problem. We'll do it another time."

He was hugely apologetic about keeping her up too late, of serving a meal that left a great deal to be desired, about driving a car that had seen better days. Her heart ached for a man who was trying so hard. He deserved to find love. But she wasn't the one. The most she could do was wish him well. Anything else would be as unfair to him as it was to her.

Less than an hour later, she climbed into her bed, incredibly weary and feeling so alone her breastbone throbbed with it. Donnie was tucked under the covers in his own room; the newlyweds were likewise tucked in for the night.

Charity drifted off into slumber, wishing...

And that's when he came to her.

The first brush of Garrett's kiss was like thistledown across her lips, a tentative touch filled with promise and overflowing with memories. How was it she recalled so distinctly the flavor of him, the texture of his skin, his musky, masculine scent? Did the recollections come from today—or had they always been with her? A part of her psyche?

Warm night air caressed her bare arms. Or was it his breath she felt skimming over her flesh? Her passion built, making her ache for him to kiss her there, on her breasts where her nipples pebbled. Kiss her everywhere. Her skin hummed with each flowing stroke of his palm, like warm water cascading over a mountain cliff, powerful in its journey, churning the depths of her need.

She sighed, turning to gain better access to his hard body, his long, powerful limbs, that part of him designed to give her such pleasure. Her heart thrust against her ribs. Her soft moans rose in volume. Or perhaps the sound was his cry of pleasure.

Then suddenly he was gone. Evaporated. She couldn't find him. She thrashed from side to side.

But he had to be there. She'd touched him, kissed him. Tasted him.

Panic spiraled through her chest. She twisted on the bed in search of the solid breadth of his body, his heat.

"Gar...rett," she sobbed.

At the sound of her own voice, she shot upright.

Morning sun flooded her bedroom; the sheet was tangled around her body, capturing her. Sweat dampened her skin.

From the adjacent room, she heard feminine moans and Bud's more guttural response.

She covered her ears and lowered her head to rest on her upraised knees. "Oh, God...please. I don't want to hear." Her body still pulsated with the memory of Garrett. Of the dream. Of the past.

Of the bleak expanse of her future.

Even worse, she didn't want to consider that Hailey had once made those sounds of pleasure in Garrett's arms.

HURRYING ACROSS the parking lot, Charity entered the candy-factory lobby slightly out of breath.

She'd gotten a call yesterday—a week after Bud's return from his honeymoon—saying that Mr. Keeley wanted to see her. She was scarcely in a position to refuse his request. If she didn't get her contract renewed for next year with the school district to handle the senior pictures, there'd be no budget for the new car she needed. Just paying the insurance on the old one would tap her out. No doubt about it, Douglas Keeley was the key to landing that contract. Certainly Maynard Grazer, president of the school board, would be no help, not with the distraction of his daughter, Jordan, having skipped out on her wedding and still listed among the missing.

The receptionist at the front counter glanced up. "May I help you?"

"Yes, I have an appointment with Mr. Keeley. I'm Charity Arden."

The blond woman's brows rose ever so slightly. "Would your appointment be with Douglas Keeley...or Garrett Keeley?"

"Garrett's here? Working?" she asked in surprise.

"I believe he is. Would you like me to check?"

"No, that's all right." Seeing Garrett now, or anytime, was not a good idea. "I'm sure my appointment must be with Mr....the senior Keeley."

The receptionist sniffed disdainfully. "I'll speak to his secretary."

While she waited for the receptionist to grant her entry to the inner sanctum, Charity fidgeted with her purse, then studied a broken fingernail, her thoughts wandering. Poor Hailey was trying desperately to be a good farmer's wife, but Charity found her sister-in-law had few domestic skills and little practical experience. Bud seemed perfectly happy, however. Apparently whatever was going on in the bedroom between them was enough to keep a smile on his face.

She sighed. At least she hadn't had a repeat of her own all too vivid dream of Garrett making love to her.

But she remained uncomfortable and on edge living in the confines of a house where two lovebirds reigned in supreme happiness. If she ever won the lottery—an unlikely possibility since she never bought a ticket—she'd spend the money to build a separate house for Bud and his bride.

The interior door of the lobby opened. Charity glanced in that direction as Garrett appeared.

A smile kicked up the corners of his mouth. "Your appointment is with me. Won't you come in?"

Her lungs seized momentarily and refused to pump any oxygen to her brain, making her feel light-headed. He was wearing a jade, zipper-front sport shirt that deepened the green of his eyes; his pleated dress slacks looked like they were hand tailored, smoothing over his pelvis without any sign of strain. He looked wonderful and sexy and devastatingly handsome in a casual, man-about-town way. She hadn't realized how much she'd missed seeing him, or how much she had wanted to.

And wondered why on earth he'd had some woman call her to make an appointment.

"I have a proposition for you," he said, opening the door a little wider when she didn't budge from her spot by the reception desk. "Why don't we talk about it in my office?"

His suggestion propelled her forward even as her cheeks heated with embarrassment. Vaguely she was aware of the receptionist's disapproving scowl as she slid past Garrett into the hallway.

"*Proposition?*" she hissed. "What the devil are you talking about?"

"A business proposition, of course. What else would I be talking about?" Looking smug, he took her elbow to escort her up a flight of stairs.

She jerked it back. "I thought I was here to see your father."

"Nope. I'm in charge of this particular project."

"You're working here now?"

"Temporarily. Trying to implement a few ideas of my own while I'm in between quarterbacking jobs."

Charity had never imagined Garrett would give up his football career to work for his father. Not even temporarily. She had the oddest feeling in the pit of her stomach he was up to no good. It was the same feeling she got when Donnie was about to commit some major mischief. Her son's eyes, she realized, twinkled in the same devilish way as Garrett's were flashing now.

His office was on the north side of the building without much of a view and was sparsely furnished with a walnut desk, leather chair and a credenza below the window. Charity noted the absence of any books and a desktop entirely bare except for the company Christmas catalog and a stapled set of papers.

He whipped the executive chair around in front of the desk. "I haven't gotten settled in yet," he said, offering her the chair. He looked pleased as punch about something as he leaned against the edge of the desk and crossed his ankles.

She squirmed uneasily in the big chair. Surely he didn't want her advice on decorating his office.

His gaze swept over her, lingering a moment on the prim collar of her cotton blouse before dipping lower to the drape of her skirt over her knees. He was undressing her. Stripping her. And her body reacted with an inner clenching she couldn't prevent.

''What is it you want, Garrett?''

Exactly what you think I want. His eyes telegraphed the thought as clearly as if the words had been spoken.

''I want to hire you as the official Fun House Candy Company catalog photographer,'' he said.

Her jaw went slack. Before she could shift mental gears—and admit she'd been reading her own mind, not Garrett's—he handed her the Christmas catalog, last year's edition, she realized.

''We've been using this guy from San Francisco. He charges us an arm and a leg, and we have to pay his lodging and meals for a week every time he comes to town to do a shoot. I figure we can save a bundle for the company by hiring local talent.''

She stared at him in amazement. ''Are you serious?''

''Yep. I've got the contract right here. Our attorney wrote it up yesterday.''

When she got a glimpse of the dollar figure on the bottom line, she gasped. ''You can't...I mean...does your father know?'' Douglas Keeley would never agree—

''I'm authorized to sign the contract. In fact, I already have, a guaranteed three-year deal with an option clause for the next three. All we need now is your name on the dotted line.''

Stunned, she gripped the contract in one hand, the catalog in the other, myriad thoughts racing through her head.

A contract like this would stabilize her income.

She'd be able to buy Donnie the bike he'd been wanting.

And the new, automated sprinklers for the pig parlor.

She'd even be able to move out, if she wanted, leaving the farm to the newlyweds.

Jumbled among her other thoughts, to her dismay, was her secret, traitorous wish that Garrett's proposition had been about an entirely different topic.

She shuddered, physically resisting that final thought.

"Do I have to sign now?" she asked. "Or can I take a little time to look over the terms of the agreement?"

His cocky smile dissolved, and he looked disappointed she hadn't leaped at his proposal. "Take as much time as you need. It's strictly a business deal."

To her great regret, though she tried not to admit that even to herself.

She thumbed through the catalog. Still life pictures of candy weren't that hard to photograph. It was simply a question of arrangements and lighting. Her imagination triggered, and she wondered—

"What would you think of using live models in the catalog?" she asked. "You know, grandmothers enjoying a box of chocolates, or kids finding chocolate cartoon characters in their Christmas stockings. It would humanize the whole thing and might give people some ideas about gift giving."

His grin restored, he said, "I knew you could do the job better than that guy in San Francisco. You've got more talent in your little finger than he has in his whole body."

Like a lovesick puppy, she basked in his praise until she left Garrett's office and reached the parking lot.

Douglas Keeley confronted Charity before she reached her car. "What were you talking to my son about?"

She froze, her hands clenching into fists. "A business arrangement."

"You and I already have an agreement. If you've told Garrett—"

"I haven't said a word." She knew Douglas Keeley would claim her farm in a heartbeat if she so much as hinted about Donnie's paternity to Garrett. Which hadn't stopped Garrett from doing some guessing.

"I don't like the idea of my son having anything to do with you, do you understand?"

Her blood started to boil. It had been a hell of a long week; her level of frustration and fatigue at coping with life were at an all-time high. Or maybe she was simply sick to death of Douglas Keeley bossing her around.

"You can't dictate my life, Mr. Keeley." The heat of anger burned her cheeks. She'd be damned if she'd let this man push her around again. "Once you were able to take advantage of me because I was a kid, scared spitless and didn't know where else to turn for help. I can take care of myself now, Mr. Keeley. *And* my son."

"I don't make idle threats, Charity." His gray

eyes narrowed in warning. "And I believe in enforcing every clause in the contracts I sign. I hope I'm making myself clear."

"Perfectly. And if it's any interest to you, I intend to bid on the school district contract and *win.*" She was also going to make sure every *i* was dotted and *t* crossed in her new contract with the Fun House Candy Company. That ought to grate the hell out of the president and CEO.

She whirled and marched to her car without so much as a glance over her shoulder. It was high time she took charge of her own life. Among other things, she decided her son had a right—an absolute God-given right—to get to know the man who had fathered him. Douglas Keeley was standing in the way of that possibility.

She was still fussing and fuming about Mr. Keeley's arrogance when she got home and parked the car by the porch.

Opening the front door, she discovered her brother was apparently taking a lunch break from the factory with his bride. They were on the couch in the living room doing—

Groaning, Charity let the door slam shut. Thank goodness she'd dropped Donnie off at his friend Shaun's house for the day. This whole situation was getting to be too much. The house was no longer hers. It now belonged to Bud and his wife. Charity was always catching them somewhere, cuddling and kissing—or worse, making her envious and snarly with her own frustration. As much as she loved the farm and had sacrificed for this small parcel of land, she wanted to be somewhere else.

THAT AFTERNOON, Garrett walked the two blocks from his house to the town square to pick up some fresh-baked bread at the bakery. He'd forgotten he'd have to endure the proprietor's daily practice session on the oboe in preparation for the summer band concerts in the park. Moe Riley's tone on the instrument compared unfavorably with a goose suffering from a sore throat.

He'd barely escaped the bakery with his hearing intact when he spotted Charity sitting on the sparkling white glider on the lawn of the town square. She had a newspaper clutched in her hands and was reading something with great interest.

Garrett approached her cautiously. He'd expected her to jump at his idea of hiring her as the Fun House resident photographer. She'd been kind of lukewarm until she'd come up with that brilliant concept of including people in the shots, not simply the candy. Garrett wondered why no one else had thought of that.

He wondered, too, why he hadn't been able to get Charity out of his mind for the past ten days. Or why the insistent thought that he was Donnie's father kept niggling at him. Outside of throwing the kid to the ground and taking a blood sample on his own, it seemed unlikely he would ever know for sure about the boy's paternity. And maybe he shouldn't concern himself.

Except he couldn't seem to let it go—let *her* go.

Hell of a thing to admit for a man who'd been set to marry another woman only ten days ago. Clearly he was romantically impaired.

"Hi, there," he said, sidling up to her. "What local gossip is so engrossing in the *Gazette* today?"

She collapsed the paper in a wad. "Nothing, really."

"You sure were intense. No hatchet killings on the front page?"

She shuddered. "Don't even think about it. Grazer's Corners is supposed to be a safe place to live."

Having sat down next to her, he extended his arm along the back of the glider. The park was pretty quiet at this hour. A couple of high-school jocks were wandering across the way; a dog was sniffing a bed of petunias, his owner distracted by a conversation with the town's barber. Three youngsters had turned the park's bandstand into a jungle gym, or maybe a spaceship.

With a shove of his foot, Garrett set the glider they were sitting on in motion. It creaked in an alternating rhythm with the flap of the flag at the top of the nearby pole.

"So if you aren't into heinous crimes, what are you reading?" he asked.

"The Want ads."

He frowned. "I already offered you a job. If the pay's not enough—"

"No. I'm looking for an apartment, or more likely a small house. For Donnie and me. I need something big enough to have a darkroom, too."

That news struck him right in the gut. "You're leaving the farm?"

"Bud and Hailey..." Color flushed her cheeks. "They don't need me around."

Garrett swore under his breath. Charity's brother was shoving her out of the house she loved, off the farm she loved, for what? For sex! he guessed. Hell, did the guy need an audience?

Impulsively—or maybe he'd planned it since the day he'd given Charity a tour of his house—he said, "Move in with me."

Only the flapping flag snapping in the wind fifty feet above them broke the silence as Charity stared at him.

Aw, hell, Garrett thought. He'd blown it. "If you need a place, I mean. You and Donnie. Both of you. You saw my house. I'm rattling around in there by myself, it's so huge. There's plenty of room for your photography stuff. You could even pay rent, if you wanted. To make you feel better, I mean. I'm not asking you to—"

"Yes."

Now it was his turn to stare at her incredulously. "You mean it?"

"On a trial basis. We'll see how it goes." She pulled her braid to the front of her shoulder.

"That's great. Really great." A grin started that he had no power to suppress, and he took her braid, pulled it behind her shoulder, giving it a friendly tug. What he really wanted to do was loosen that braid and have those long, silken strands draped over his naked chest. He doubted she'd be pleased with that thought.

She eyed him warily. "I'm going to pay you rent. This is strictly business. Like the catalog contract I've decided to sign. Okay?"

"Fine by me." He swallowed hard and tried to remain cool, but he felt like he had the ball on the fifty-yard line, thirty seconds to play and the team was down by six points. His adrenaline whipped through his body at a million miles per hour. "When did you think you might want to move in?"

"Would this evening be too soon?"

Garrett could have jumped up and clicked his heels together—or tossed a perfect pass into the end zone—except he suspected Charity would back out of the deal in a flash if she had any idea of his ulterior motives.

But he was going to have her in his house. Donnie, too. Somehow he'd get to the bottom of the mystery of the child's paternity. And explore his feelings for Charity in the process.

Not a bad deal, he thought. Not bad at all.

Chapter Eight

"You can't move in with Garrett."

Bud loomed over Charity, glowering at her as she tossed a nightgown and some underwear into her suitcase. She wouldn't call any of her lingerie alluring. In fact, she might want to think about remedying that situation—if she got up the nerve. But one impulsive decision per day was pretty much her quota. Moving in with Garrett was the first and only step she was taking for now.

As much as she might tell herself that her move was motivated by the need to escape an awkward situation at home with Bud and his bride, Charity had to admit another, less rational reason. No matter how much she feared losing the farm, or that Garrett might find out about their son, she simply wanted to be near him.

And she chided herself for such foolish risks. "You're making it sound like I'm doing something sinful," she said. "I'm renting a room—rooms—for myself and my son in a house that's too big for one person, and Garrett's all alone, as you no doubt recall." She cocked an eyebrow in the silent suggestion her brother was at least in part responsible for

Garrett's empty house. "What's so awful about that?"

"What it will do to your reputation, that's what's so awful. I never thought when I brought Garrett here... I mean, this is a small town. There'll be talk. If you're going to get together with Garrett, he ought to—"

"Ought to what? I'm an unwed mother, Bud. How much worse could my reputation be?" She picked up a sweater, shook it out, then put it back in the drawer. The weather would be too warm for wool for a long time yet. She couldn't begin to plan that far ahead.

"Nobody's ever thought you were a tramp."

"How kind of you to say so."

"Aw, sis, you know what I mean. People will think that, well, that you're sleeping with Garrett."

"They can think whatever they want." Maybe she would sleep with Garrett—and maybe she wouldn't. She was tired of people like Douglas Keeley and her well-meaning brother telling her how she should live her life. She knew in the long term she didn't have any future with Garrett, but maybe as a temporary arrangement—

"Bud, listen to me. My moving out is the best thing that could happen to you and Hailey. You'll have a chance to really get acquainted without Donnie and me underfoot. And she can learn how to cook and handle the chores around the farm without always comparing herself to me."

He looked stunned. "Are we the reason you're moving out? You love the farm, Charity. You shouldn't have to—"

She wrapped her arms around his midsection and

hugged him. "Just trust me on this, Bud. I need to go. At least for a while. The reasons don't matter." They weren't even entirely clear in her own mind. Or maybe she simply didn't want to admit the depth of her feelings. *Or her frustrations.*

"I'm telling you, sis, if he does anything—*anything*—to hurt you, I'll personally break both of his kneecaps. Permanently. Got that?"

"I love you, too, Bud." Tears suddenly blurred her vision. So much in her life had changed in the past ten days, and yet her brother was still a constant. She knew for a fact he wouldn't have intentionally forced her to move from the farm or made her feel uncomfortable in her own home. She had to do this for herself—and for her son. "You're the best brother a girl ever had."

"Yeah, well, I'm not so sure about that. But you're all right, sis. I just want you to be happy. Hailey does, too." He gave her an awkward hug, then stepped back. "Whatever I've done, I never meant to mess up your life."

"Don't be too nice to me. Donnie and I might move back home faster than you'd like." Especially if she lost her nerve—which remained a strong possibility.

He chuckled. "I still can't figure Garrett letting you move in, I mean if you're not sleeping with him. It's gotta cramp his style to have a woman in the house—"

"Let's not discuss Garrett's love life, huh?" She hadn't given any thought to another woman in Garrett's life and didn't want to consider it now. "If he had his way, he'd be picked up by an NFL team tomorrow and be at training camp by dinnertime."

Then he'd be back in his element with all the groupies who thrived on the vicarious thrill of hanging around with a celebrity. *And* going to bed with him, she thought with a heart-stopping rush of jealousy. "With any luck, Donnie and I will have that whole big house to ourselves."

Bud didn't exactly look like he'd bought her flippant response. Nor did she. She would simply have to grit her teeth and see what happened.

"WAY COOL, MOM." Grinning, Donnie was flat on his back, spread-eagled on the big bed he'd chosen for his own. He waved his outstretched arms up and down as if he were making a snow angel on the elegant handmade quilt. "Wait till Shaun hears about this."

"You aren't going to get lost in there, are you?" Charity asked.

"Uh-uh. There's even lots of room for—" Tensing, he shot a troubled glance at Garrett.

Realizing what her son was thinking, Charity said, "Donnie has a special friend named Bob-Bob, who nobody else can see. Bob-Bob sometimes gets into mischief and tries to blame Donnie, but usually he's well behaved. As long as he doesn't get too wild, we kind of like to have him around. If you don't mind." She gave Garrett an imploring look.

The corners of Garrett's lips kicked up. He shrugged. "Hey, I had a friend like that. I called him—" a thoughtful frown lowered his brows "—Arnold? No, Arnie! I remember. Man, that guy used to get me into so much trouble. Donnie, you tell your buddy if he's square with us he can stick around as long as he likes."

Donnie visibly relaxed, hopping up off the bed to explore the rest of the room. "It's okay," he said, peering into the walk-in closet. "I've almost outgrown Bob-Bob anyways."

Charity could have kissed Garrett. Her son's imaginary friend had been a bone of contention with Bud, who'd never had a need for anything except tools and tractors and engines to take apart. In contrast, Charity had expressed her creativity with a paintbrush—until reality had set in and she'd had to find a way to support her child.

"Come on, you guys," Garrett said. His hand brushed across the back of Charity's shoulders in an invitation. "I got us Chinese takeout for dinner. It's keeping warm in the oven. We mess around much longer, and the cardboard cartons are gonna be charcoal."

In the kitchen, Garrett used a couple of old hot pads to haul the cartons of chow mein and sweet-and-sour pork out of the oven and placed them on the table with the other containers. His nerves were jumping and knotting in his gut. They always did that before a big game. An important game. He'd hang out in the locker room, sweating, trying to look confident, plays running through his head. Strategies.

The game plan he needed now wasn't in any playbook. At least not any he had read.

Damn, he wasn't even sure what would constitute a win in this case. Simply getting Charity into his bed would seem like a shallow victory—though he wanted that more than he'd wanted a woman since that first time they'd made love at the lake. The only time.

He eyed Donnie, who was kneeling on his chair at the table peering into the food cartons. The timing of that lake picnic was just about perfect....

"Where are the plates?" Charity asked.

He jumped. "To the right of the sink," he answered. *She'd never returned his calls eight years ago.* Why the hell not?

"Can we use chopsticks, Mom?"

"If Garrett doesn't mind if half your dinner ends up on the floor." She shot Garrett a smile that made his knees go weak.

She's here now.

"No problem," he said. "If the mess gets too deep, we'll shovel it out like the pig parlor."

"Yeah, Mom. Or we can squirt a hose in here 'n' wash the glop out the back door."

"Wonderful." Laughing, she rolled her eyes. "I can see I'm outnumbered when it comes to domestic talents. Next thing I know, you'll want me to stand you both in a checkers game."

"You'd lose, Mom. Garrett's almost as good as me."

As she placed the plates on the table, she met his gaze. Warm brown eyes a man could happily drown in. Eyes that offered love to a man who could find the key to her heart.

He suddenly, desperately wanted to be that man.

"Not an ounce of modesty there," she said softly. "Must run in his genes."

Charity's genes? Or his own? Garrett wondered.

"You've always seemed pretty modest about your accomplishments." He scooped out a spoonful of chicken chow mein for Donnie, then served Charity as she sat down opposite him, next to her son. The kitchen table might be oak but it was so scarred from years of use, it was nothing to write home about. But sitting here with Charity and her son, it felt like home.

"I've never had much of anything to brag about," she said, serving herself from the carton of sweet and sour. "Except for Donnie." She sent her son a loving look, watching as he struggled to master even one bite of food with his chopsticks. "I never even graduated from high school."

"You didn't?" That shocked the hell out of Garrett.

Donnie piped up. "I'm gonna go to college on a soccer scholarship and then I'm gonna be an astronaut." His efforts with his chopsticks suggested his small-muscle coordination wasn't yet fully developed.

"I missed most of my senior year," Charity said. "I got my GED instead."

Now, why had she done that? Garrett wondered. She was smart. He recalled she'd been thinking of going to an art college. No reason why she should have dropped out of school.

Slowly, his chopsticks in mid-flight, his gaze slid to Donnie. *Except to have a baby.*

"My grandfather had a stroke at the beginning of my senior year," she continued, distracting him from the thought. "Grandma was having an awful time trying to take care of him and keep up with the farmwork, too. Plus pay the bills." She expertly snared a piece of pork with her chopsticks. "So I stayed home."

"Bud couldn't help out?"

"He was at Cal Poly. We didn't want him to miss out on his education."

"But it was okay for you to quit school?" he asked, astonished at such a sexist attitude that had a woman dropping out of high school while her brother kept working toward his college degree.

"It was the right thing to do. Bud had to drop out later anyway. At least he finished three years, and that helped him get the job at the factory."

Oh, man, there was something going on here she wasn't telling him. And what she *had* told him was gnawing away at him. Her sacrifices. The burdens she'd carried.

God, had it been his fault? Guilt burrowed into his gut.

The overhead lights cast provocative shadows across Charity's face, highlighting the sculpted shape of her cheeks, her straight nose, the strong shape of her jaw. She had her hair pulled back and braided, as though she was determined to control the flyaway curls...and had failed. They feathered her cheeks, softening her features and making her look ever more feminine. Appealing.

She was wearing a short T-top that edged up from her jeans when she moved, revealing a line of tanned flesh at her midriff. Her skin looked as soft and inviting as satin sheets, and that's exactly where she ought to be. On *his* satin sheets—if he had any.

Garrett could hardly keep his eyes off of her.

And with a fair amount of masculine satisfaction, he noted her glances toward him. Interested glances, sometimes beneath her golden brown, lowered lashes. Looks that set his libido on edge. On fire. *Strictly business, hell!*

Never in his life had he been so far from thinking about business. The roof could cave in and he wouldn't notice. He only had eyes for Charity.

His pulse moved restlessly at his temple—and throbbed painfully far lower in his body. He was alternately hot and cold, an adolescent on the make. Sweat formed on the ridge of his back. Swallowing became an act of sheer willpower.

"What are these things?" Donnie asked, holding up a bean sprout between his chopsticks.

"White worms," Garrett answered. "They make your muscles grow."

"Hey, neat," the boy said. He plopped one into his mouth.

Charity's smile brought a sparkle to her eyes that was as bright as the floodlights in the old Jack Murphy Stadium. And all that candlepower was meant for him.

Little wonder he had trouble getting through dinner and the cleanup that followed. Or that he lost two checkers games to Donnie in record time. He had a lot of other things on his mind. Strictly business wasn't one of them.

CHARITY RETURNED from upstairs after putting Donnie to bed. She found Garrett pacing the living room, looking like a caged animal. Tension radiated from him with each long-legged stride, mirroring the anticipation that hummed through her like electricity through high-voltage power lines. Barefoot, he was wearing running shorts and a 49ers T-shirt. His muscular legs, covered with a thatch of blond hair, flexed with each step he took; a curved purple scar on his left knee marked his recent surgery. She ached with sympathy that the small flaw could spell the end of the career he'd worked so hard to achieve.

He turned when she entered the room. "Donnie all set?"

"He's fine. He's very excited to be here." So was she, though she wasn't all that sure her nerves would hold out. "You didn't have to arrange dinner for us. That wasn't part of the deal."

He shrugged. "I hate to eat alone."

"Hmm." She couldn't recall the last time she'd eaten alone. There'd always been Bud and Donnie, at one time her grandparents, too.

Shifting her weight from one foot to the other, she felt at loose ends, not knowing quite what to say or do.

"You want to sit outside?" he asked. "There's a swing on the porch."

"You don't have to entertain me, Garrett. I'm a tenant, remember?"

"I could use the company." His direct gaze did something wild and hot to her midsection. Something very nearly irresistible.

Fresh air sounded like a timely idea. Her lungs kept seizing; her heart beat erratically as though she were running uphill in the high Sierras and starved for oxygen. Feeling light-headed, she pressed out through the screen door and drew a deep breath. It did little to settle her nerves. *Would he make love to her tonight? Should she be the aggressor? Or wait for him to make a move? Assuming he even wanted to. And her nerve didn't fail her.*

A warm evening breeze rustled the leaves of a

poplar tree in the front yard and carried with it the scent of roses and freshly mowed grass. Crickets were tuning up their instruments in search of romance. In the distance, there was a car heading toward the highway.

The light from the living room cast Garrett's shadow across the porch as he followed her outside. Big and tall and larger than life. Dominating the outdoors as he had the space inside the house.

She sat on the swing and started it moving with a shove of her sandal. Her fingers twisted in her lap.

"I hope I'm not cramping your style by moving in on you." In spite of the nervous tightening of her throat, her voice remained calm, not disturbing the silence.

He leaned his hips against the porch railing, his hand resting on one of the posts. "My style?"

"You have a reputation with the ladies. If you ever need privacy—"

"Being a quarterback tends to draw a crowd, including women," he admitted. "They vanish just as fast when you're down on your luck."

"Do you miss them?"

In the dim light, she saw the quick flash of his smile. "I prefer my current company, thanks."

Her heart took another stuttering beat, and she pushed a little harder with her foot. The chains creaked. Lights were on in the houses up and down the block, but little sound escaped. Several cars were parked along the curb beneath the old oak trees that lined the street.

Garrett shoved away from the railing and crossed the porch to sit next to Charity. His weight tilted the swing and set it rocking again.

"After that night at the lake, why didn't you return my phone calls?"

Her thoughts slid back to that night so long ago, the way he had held her, kissed her, made love to her, her uninhibited response to everything that had happened between them. "I was embarrassed about what I'd done," she answered honestly. "You were a big man on campus—a college campus, not even just high school—and I was a kid. I felt like I'd made a fool of myself."

"You hadn't. I wanted you to know that before I went back to school. I wanted to see you again."

A band tightened around her chest. "I was afraid you thought I was a tramp. I mean, I hardly knew you and still I let you—"

"I knew you weren't easy, Charity. I'd seen you around town."

"You had?"

"That summer you were working at Harmon's Department Store in the men's department. I came in looking for a jockstrap and you were the only one who was around. You blushed like crazy when you sold it to me."

Chuckling softly, she blushed again and probably even more brightly than she had as a seventeen-year-old. She'd been such a fool, stammering as she'd asked him what size he needed. Later that summer, she'd found out if there'd been a choice, large would have been the answer. "I remember. I think you blushed, too."

"Naw. Jocks aren't allowed. It's in the contract we sign when we get our first Nerf ball."

In spite of herself, she smiled. "You're more than a jock, you know."

His arm slid around the back of the swing, his fingers idly sculpting the curve of her shoulder. "Whatever gave you that idea?"

"You graduated from college and were an Academic All-American. That's nothing to sneeze at."

"How'd you know that?"

She shrugged. "The *Grazer Gazette* made a big deal about it."

"Oh, yeah. Dad sent me the clipping." He leaned toward her to brush a kiss to her temple.

Heated goose bumps sped down her spine. "Garrett..."

"Yes, cinnamon girl." The raspy thickness in his voice sent a coil of desire right to her midsection. "Tell me what you want." His lips brushed her temple again, his fingers stroked the column of her neck.

She wanted him—Garrett—the man she'd loved for as long as she could remember. But after all these years of denying her feelings, did she have the nerve to grab the golden ring, particularly when she doubted she'd be able to hold on to it for long? Not if he got picked up by another football team. Not if someone as beautiful and sexy as Hailey came along. Not if Douglas Keeley found out.

A bright light and feminine laughter from the neighbor's house across the street saved her from answering those questions. And drove every ounce of courage from her soul. Apparently a meeting of the Grazer's Corners Reading Club was just breaking up, and Agatha Flintstone and a number of other notable ladies of the community were leaving for home.

Charity shot to her feet like a spring in the old swing had goosed her. She and Garrett might as well have taken out an ad in the *Gazette*; the whole town would know by morning that she'd been spotted at his house.

"I'd better turn in. Donnie's an early riser." The words spilled out breathlessly. "He's got a soccer game tomorrow, and I'm supposed to bring the oranges for the halftime snack."

"Really? I'd like to see him play. Mind if I come along?"

"No, that'd be fine." She backed toward the door. Dear Lord, it was getting harder and harder not to blurt out the truth, that Garrett was Donnie's father. A truth Charity could never dare admit. "He'd like that, I'm sure."

Like a coward, she fled into the house and up the stairs to her room. What on earth had she been thinking? She wasn't the kind of woman who simply moved in with a man—*slept* with him. Bud had been right. She didn't want to be the talk of the town. She'd gone through that once, when she'd been pregnant and unmarried.

Now she had her son to worry about.

But how could she go home and endure the passionate duet that went on in the very next room?

How could she deny herself the chance to be in Garrett's arms again, if only for a little while?

GARRETT STOOD on the front porch, listening to the women departing across the street, and wondering what the hell had gone wrong. Something about his sex appeal must be sorely lacking these days. His bride had walked out on him, and Charity, who he knew damn well was attracted to him, had given him another brush-off.

He'd heard her quick intake of air when he'd kissed her. She'd been affected, dammit! Though not nearly as much as he'd been by what had only been a hint of a kiss. He still wouldn't want to go anywhere where the lights were bright, not while his jogging shorts were stretched out in proof of how much she affected him.

No woman had ever confused him as much as Charity did, either. She'd slept with him once—a long time ago; now she'd moved in with him, albeit as a boarder. But she backpedaled whenever he pressed too hard. Which ought to give him a clue.

Patience had never been Garrett's long suit. Clenching his teeth, he decided he'd have to give her some space and a little time. Not much, he thought grimly. He couldn't stay on this erotic roller coaster too long or he'd explode.

CHARITY WALKED across the school grounds toward the grassy field that had been marked off for soccer, goals placed at either end. Donnie, as usual, had run on ahead to join his teammates. Sauntering beside her, wearing walking shorts and a T-shirt that showed off his well-defined physique, Garrett looked for all the world like a proud father who'd come to see his son play.

Except he was still in the dark that Donnie actually was his son.

Lord, Charity hated that she'd been forced to lie—not only to Garrett but to her son, as well. So far Donnie hadn't asked too many questions about his father. But some day he would.

The sun was already warm, and Charity began to

sweat. *What tangled webs we mortals weave,* she thought bleakly.

"Why don't you find a spot for us over there on the sideline?" she suggested to Garrett, who was carrying folding lawn chairs for them both. "I'll take the oranges to the team mother."

"You got it." With an easy stride, he veered in that direction.

She headed for the group of mothers who had gathered off to the side of the midfield line where the ice chest and equipment bag had been left. The ladies were chatting with a good deal of animation, and their laughter filled the air.

Smiling, Charity joined the crowd.

Suddenly everyone went quiet. The instant silence was nearly deafening. It was like her arrival had put a cork in a bottle of carbonated water and stopped the fizz.

"Hi, everyone," she said, ignoring the shimmer of unease that traveled up her spine. She placed the oranges on the ice chest.

"Hi, Charity," Mollie Tarrant cooed.

"'Morning, honey, you're lookin' fine this morning," Beth Stover said in a tone that gave Charity the feeling she was being inspected for lice—or evidence of a sexually transmitted disease.

The others chorused their greetings, then drifted off to re-form in smaller gatherings of twos and threes. Only Dorothy Ritters, Shaun's mother, remained.

"Why is it I feel like I broke up a first-class gossip session?" Charity asked. "And the topic was me."

Dot laughed and gave her a quick hug. A large

woman, she always embraced her friends with enthusiasm and an open heart. "Must be because you're so perceptive."

"What did I do wrong now?" As if Charity wasn't quite sure the topic included Garrett Keeley's name.

"Oh, nothing, hon. Except bring a big, tall hunk of a man to the game with you. A man who was recently dumped by his bride and is once again an available, to-die-for bachelor. And there's a rumor going around you're pretty wrapped up in him."

Charity grimaced. *Agatha Flintstone must have a telegraph system that covers the whole town!* "I'm renting rooms in his house. That's all."

Dot's pixie-cut hair fluffed up as she shook her head. Her dark eyes sparkled. "That's one I haven't heard. Now the guys are *charging* women to move in with them?"

"No, that's not what they're doing. I needed a place to live. Bud and Hailey are so lovey-dovey it was driving me crazy, and I was a little afraid Donnie might walk in on an X-rated scene. Garrett was kind enough to offer his home—temporarily. Okay?"

"Okay by me." Dot opened the ice chest and dropped the oranges in next to the bottled water. "There's also talk that Garrett has been checking birth records at city hall—records from about seven years ago. Don't suppose you'd know why he'd be doing that?"

Charity felt all the blood drain from her face. For a moment she was sure she was having a heat stroke. He couldn't have found out anything. He *couldn't.*

But he'd been looking, and that was dangerous. Terrifying, she realized.

Mr. Keeley could make good on his threat to call in the loan if he even suspected she'd told Garrett the truth. She'd lose the farm for Bud and Hailey and herself, as well as for her son. In spite of the fact Hailey's family had money, it seemed unlikely her parents would step forward to save the pig farm from foreclosure, not when they disapproved of their daughter's choice of a husband.

Dot touched Charity lightly on the arm. "Look, hon, I don't know what's going on but I do know you deserve happiness. If it was me and I had a chance to land a hunk like Garrett Keeley, no amount of gossip in the world would stop me. Of course," she said with a robust laugh, "my hubby might object. He's funny about things like that."

"My moving into Garrett's house is strictly a business arrangement," Charity reiterated. "Besides, whatever the gossips might be saying, I'm not Garrett's type."

"No? I wouldn't be so sure about that. He sure keeps looking this direction, and I don't think it's me he's eyeing."

Charity's gaze swept toward Garrett, and her breath lodged in her lungs. He was looking at her, all right, and there was a hunger in his eyes that was readable from half the length of the soccer field.

She wanted to tell him to stop, to not let others see his blatant masculine interest, to not fuel the gossip any more than they already had.

But she couldn't. She was too thrilled by the possibility she might actually be his type.

Chapter Nine

The ball popped out of the gaggle of seven-year-olds, and three boys raced toward the goal, the defenders backpedaling as fast as they could go.

"Shoot, Donnie! Shoot!" Garrett shouted, caught up in the game. A defender got in the boy's way, but Donnie managed to get around him. The goalie jockeyed to cut off the angle. "Now, son! Boot it in there!"

Donnie slammed the ball at the goal. Just missing, the ball caromed off the goalpost and dribbled back toward the middle of the field. The goalie made a dive for it; Donnie executed a hook slide that caught the ball, sailing it into the corner of the net.

"Score! Way to go!" Garrett pumped his fist in the air.

The moms and dads rooting for the blue-and-white team cheered; across the way the parents groaned.

Drained, Garrett collapsed back into his chair. "Man, this being a fan is hard work." He grinned at Charity, who'd been on her feet cheering for most of the game. Her cheeks glowed as pink as a sunrise and were sheened with perspiration like morning dew on a rose petal. Damp curls framed her face.

Breathing deeply and returning his smile, she covered her heart with her hand as she sat down. "You have no idea how hard this athletic stuff is on a mom. I swear, I don't think I'll be able to take it if he decides to play football."

"Come to think of it, my mother rarely came to any of my games." He took Charity's hand, rubbing his thumb across her knuckles. They were the hands of an artist but also those of a woman who was used to hard work, her nails cut short and the white line of an old scar on her index finger. She deserved to wear nail polish and diamond rings.

He wanted to feel her hands on him.

"Maybe I misjudged my mom. Maybe she didn't come to my games because she didn't like to watch me get creamed."

Slowly she withdrew her hand. Her tongue darted out to moisten her lips, and Garrett felt the gesture clear down in his shorts. "You're probably right," she said, her voice a husky whisper.

A shout went up from the opposite side of the field, drawing Garrett's reluctant attention back to the game. He was sitting six inches away from Charity and he wanted to touch her so badly it hurt. Hell, he wanted to make love to her right here on the grass in the bright light of day. Not exactly an appropriate thing to be thinking about at her kid's soccer game. His body, however, didn't make any fine distinctions about what would be seemly.

When the first half came to an end, Charity said, "I've got to go help Dot and the kids with the oranges. You don't have to stick around for the second half if you don't want to. I'm sure someone could drive us—"

"I'm not that easy to get rid of, Charity. I'll be here."

She blinked and drew a breath that lifted her T-shirt, then turned to walk to the spot where the team had gathered. The sexy sway of her hips just about undid Garrett.

"You always did have an eye for a pretty girl."

Garrett grinned in recognition of his old coach's voice. "Hey there, Coach Riddler." As he extended his hand, Garrett noted Riddler's gray hair had thinned considerably since the last time he had seen his high-school mentor, and age spots had darkened splotches on his forehead. The paunch around his middle had expanded, too. "Don't tell me they've got you coaching midget soccer now."

"Not likely. My grandson's playing." He rubbed his left arm, grimacing slightly as if he had strained a muscle. "My daughter had to work this morning, so I got to bring the boy. Too bad his team is losing."

"Funny, this side of the field thinks it's okay." And Charity's boy, Donnie, had scored the goal that had them in the lead. "So what are the prospects for Grazer High's football team this year?"

"We've got five starters returning and there's a good-lookin' bunch of boys coming up from the JVs. I think we'll do okay."

"Always the optimist, huh?"

"Doesn't pay to be otherwise. Fact is, though, I'm getting old. One more season..."

"They'd never be able to replace you, Coach."

"My shoes aren't that big. All it takes is someone

who cares about the youngsters." Riddler narrowed his gray eyes, honing in on Garrett like he used to do when he'd been goofing off too much. "A man like you could do it."

"Not me, Coach, at least not for a while. I've got a few good years of playing left in me."

"Your knee's okay?"

"It will be soon enough. My agent's shopping me around now. Something will turn up."

The soccer players ran out onto the field for the beginning of the second half.

"I hope it does, son. If not, well...drop by the practice field. Some of the boys are training on their own before the season starts. They could use a little experienced guidance."

"Sure, Coach, I'll do that." They shook hands again, and the coach headed around the end of the field, his pace slower than Garrett remembered. But then it had been nearly fifteen years since he attended Grazer High. Everybody gets old sometime. He just hated to see it happen to Coach.

But he didn't intend to follow in Riddler's footsteps anytime soon. With a mended knee, he ought to have five more good years as an active player. Dammit, he wanted a Super Bowl ring. He wasn't ready to settle for his photo in a high-school annual standing next to a bunch of adolescent jocks.

He grinned, slanting a glance toward the woman who was sharing his house. Starring in the annual wasn't his idea of a lifetime goal even if the photographer was Charity Arden.

CHARITY LINGERED to clean up the mess the team had made with the oranges. She couldn't concentrate on the game. All she could think about was the way Garrett had held her hand, the contrast between his long tapered fingers and hers. And how she desperately wished hers hadn't looked like farmworker's hands, rough and red, with chipped fingernails. Surely he was used to women who had weekly manicures.

She'd never had one in her life.

The second half of the game was a blur. When it was over, she knew only that their team had won and Donnie had scored another goal. But the details were fuzzy, her thoughts muddled as she kept thinking about Garrett, watching him enjoy his son's performance, and thinking his pride in Donnie's accomplishments would be even greater if he knew he was the boy's father.

''Hey, Mom!'' Donnie blasted across the field toward her after the winning cheers, team handshakes and congratulations were over. ''Can I spend the night at Shaun's house? Can I, Mom? Huh? Please.''

Panic slipped through her. No way did she want to be entirely alone with Garrett. She shot a look at her traitorous friend Dot. ''Why don't you ask if Shaun can spend the night at our house?'' she asked her son. ''There's plenty of room for two in your new bed.''

''I can't, Mom. Pete and Billy are gonna stay over at Shaun's, and he's got this cool new computer game. Aliens 'n' stuff.''

Garrett walked up behind her. ''How could you possibly say no to that?'' he asked, his voice teasing.

For a couple of very good reasons, most of them related to her sanity and lack of willpower. ''I don't know, honey. I mean we've just moved in...''

Dot caught her eye. ''Everybody deserves a night off once in a while. I'll get him back home to you in the morning. Meanwhile—'' her smile resembled that of a cat that had swallowed a canary and enjoyed every morsel ''—have fun.''

''Sounds like a good plan to me,'' Garrett agreed all too readily.

Charity fumed, wanting to elbow Garrett in the ribs. And Dot, too. Some friend she was! They'd backed her into a corner, or rather she'd been sandwiched between two very determined people—a biologically compulsive matchmaker and a man whom she ought to keep at arm's length. She didn't see any way to escape.

Even worse, Charity wasn't sure she wanted to escape, though the fiery tongues of gossip would very likely turn Grazer's Corners into an inferno of speculation.

SHE SPENT THE AFTERNOON setting up her darkroom in what used to be a pantry off the kitchen in Garrett's house.

''You need any more help?'' he asked after hauling the last big cardboard box in from the car. On the way back from the farm, they'd dropped Donnie off at Shaun's house. Now it was just the two of them alone in a house that seemed to be shrinking in size.

''No, I've got it now. I just have to get things organized.''

Garrett had offered to have plumbing installed in the room and a sink to make her work easier, but she'd put him off, reminding him this was only a temporary arrangement. He hadn't looked entirely pleased with her insistence.

"If you're sure you don't need me for now, I'll go do my workout. I'm seeing the doctor next week about my knee. I want it to be as strong as possible. Maybe he'll release me to get back to work."

She eyed his muscular legs and the knee that had been so badly injured. "You've been on your feet a lot today. Shouldn't you be resting it?"

"No pain, no gain, as they say." He shoved his sun-streaked blond hair back from his forehead, the corners of his eyes crinkling as he smiled. "Call me if you need me for anything."

"I will," she promised. She exhaled softly after he left. The pantry—which was twice the size of her darkroom at home—was far too small a space to share with Garrett. They'd accidentally brushed against each other too many times; she couldn't draw a breath without catching his musky masculine scent. More than once, she'd been tempted to wrap her arms around him and place her head on his chest so she could feel the beat of his heart.

But of course, a hug would escalate into something else. Like kissing. And making love.

She swallowed hard.

It might make better sense if she locked herself in the darkroom until Donnie came home in the morning to chaperon her.

She took her time hooking up the red light outside the pantry door—the inviolate warning to others not to enter because she was developing film. Lingering a while longer, she stored her chemicals in a cupboard along with developing contact paper, until finally her need for fresh air drove her from the darkroom. She stood in the kitchen a moment listening to a steady thump-thumping sound coming from somewhere in the house. Like a fish being reeled in on a line, she was drawn to Garrett's exercise room.

He'd taken off his shirt, and rivulets of sweat edged down through the faint pattern of blond hair on his chest. Glistening, his pectorals flexed as he strained. His face twisted with pain each time he lifted his leg against the force of the weight. He looked as determined as a gladiator training to wrestle with lions. A heart-stopping sight, both gloriously masculine and poignant at the same time. He wanted his football career that much.

In the corner of the room, the light glowed red on the Jacuzzi, the water stirring gently.

"Ninety-seven, ninety-eight, ninety-nine," he murmured with each labored breath. With one last effort, he raised the weight again, then fell back on the workout bench, his eyes closed. The muscles in his legs stood out like ropes.

"Are you all right?" she asked.

He turned his head to the side, slowly perusing her with his green-eyed gaze. "Let's just say if I were at training camp, I'd be lining up for a massage about now."

"I could give you one." The impulsive offer was out of her mouth before she could snatch it back. Massaging Garrett would mean *touching* him, *caressing* him. Being so close she'd be able to *kiss* him with almost no effort at all.

"You've got yourself a deal, lady." He levered himself to his feet, wiped his face with a towel and shifted to a long padded table near the wall. He lay down on his stomach. "I'll even give you a discount on your rent for being my personal trainer."

Her throat tightened. "No charge."

"The liniment's in the cupboard."

He was taking her offer of a massage casually; she should be able to do the same. But her heart was slamming against her ribs. Her mouth felt as dry as a hundred-year drought.

She found the bottle of oil, poured some in her palms and rubbed them together. Her fingers trembled in anticipation; so did her stomach.

Tentatively she slicked her palms over his shoulders. The flesh rippled beneath her hands, alive and warm and smoothly textured. The scent of mint wafted up, the oil combining with Garrett's own masculine aroma. She pressed more firmly, using her thumbs to relax his iron-hard muscles. Against his deep, even tan, her hands looked pale. Almost fragile. And feminine.

She followed the long valley of his spine, learning the shape of each vertebra, knowing she wanted to kiss him there—between his shoulder blades—and lower, where his shorts bisected his back. She wanted to taste him, savor his flavor, indulge herself in all that was unique about Garrett Keeley.

A growing awareness of her need slid through her traitorous body, liquefying her bones.

The late-afternoon sun dappled the room, sending dust motes into the air, creating a sensual play of dark and light across his back. The perfect back of an athlete, molded by the artistry of hard work.

Her hands went lower, to his muscular thigh, tight and hard, roughened by blond hair—

With a low, feral growl, he twisted and whipped

upright to a sitting position, snaring her wrist. "Enough, cinnamon girl." His husky voice, intimate in the quiet room, paralyzed her lungs and sent her heart spiraling out of control. "Your turn."

"No, I don't want—"

"Fair's fair." His eyes, so dark they were almost black, raked over her. "You'll have to lose the shirt. And your jeans."

"Garrett, I can't—"

"Nothing's going to happen here you don't want, sweetheart. I'm going to give you a massage. That's all."

She wanted to believe him; she wanted *not* to believe him. She wanted to follow her heart.

As though she were two people, she shook her head in refusal even as she crossed her arms to tug off her shirt. His hands went to the snap on her jeans. Before she could object—or come to her senses—she'd stepped out of them. Wearing only her panties and bra, she shivered, though the room was warm.

Taking his place on the workout table, she waited for him to touch her, remembering the tactile feel of his hands, their roughness, their gentle caress. She drew a quick breath at the first stroke of his palm, so brief she almost thought she'd imagined it. Had wanted it that much.

Her dreams—her memories—came alive beneath his hands. Her blood pulsed thickly through her veins; her limbs went limp. Deep within her, a throbbing started. Heavy. Aching. Her breathing grew rapid.

His fingertips lightly brushed the sides of her

breasts. She moaned and felt the clasp on her bra come loose.

"Oh..." A sigh escaped her lips.

"You're doing fine, cinnamon girl. Just fine."

Yes, she was; no, she wasn't. She wanted more, ached for more. For too many years, she'd denied this elemental part of her, the part that only Garrett had awakened.

His hand slid under the elastic of her panties, and he squeezed gently.

Her whole body reacted with a sharp clenching of muscles, particularly those meant to grip a man and hold him within her. Hold *Garrett* within her.

When his hands skimmed over her thighs, his fingers trailing over the sensitive inner flesh, she sobbed his name. "Please, Garrett...help me."

"My pleasure, sweetheart." As if she weighed nothing at all, he turned her over and lifted her in his arms. "After a relaxing massage, there's nothing like a warm soak in a Jacuzzi."

"I'm not...relaxed."

"I'm workin' on it, sweet thing. Be patient."

In a few easy strides, he crossed the room and stepped down into the pool of warm water. He settled her on his lap, his arousal pressing against her thigh until he shifted her to an even more intimate arrangement—face-to-face, straddling him.

She was weightless and hot, the warmth of his body enveloping her, coiling around the juncture where his hard shaft met the sheer fabric of her panties. She pressed against him.

"Easy now," he said in a raspy whisper. "We don't want to go too fast."

"It's been so long...." The water swirled around her. His hands covered her—everywhere.

Lifting her arms, she cupped the back of his head and pulled him closer. His mouth tasted of heavenly heat as she plunged her tongue inside. She moved against him, the sweet friction pure bliss.

"Charity, sweetheart... You're killing me. I don't have any protection here...."

"Oh, Garrett, don't stop." Through a mental haze, she did some quick calculations. She desperately wanted Garrett, but she desperately didn't want to get into the same fix she had seven years ago, pregnant and unmarried. "It's safe. I'm..." He shifted her weight again, and she nearly came undone, groaning his name, wanting him so much she would have died rather than end this heavenly feeling.

The next thing she knew, her panties were floating free in the roiling water playing catch-me-if-you-can with Garrett's running shorts.

And then he was inside her, filling her. She rode him, panting, crying, moaning his name again as he thrust into her.

He gave a low, guttural groan that sent her over the edge. She shattered into a million brilliant pieces, the rays of the afternoon sun catching in her vision like diamonds before she closed them against the beauty—and trepidation—that enveloped her.

"SO HOW DO YOU LIKE your steak?" Garrett asked sometime later. On the way back from the farm while bringing Charity's photography stuff to his house, he'd had the foresight to stop at the grocery store for some meat and salad makings. Not the store where Homer worked, he thought with a surge of possessiveness.

"Medium, medium rare." Hugging herself, she stood at the edge of the backyard patio watching the last rays of sunlight sink into the western clouds. "Whatever's easy."

He turned the steaks on the grill. The evening air was still warm. In contrast, Charity had turned cool after their lovemaking. A bad case of guilt, he suspected. That's not how he felt.

Charity had been all he remembered, and more. He'd never known a woman who was more responsive, or one who had touched him more deeply at some basic level that went beyond sex. He wasn't yet willing to give that feeling a name. Hell, it had been only two weeks ago that he'd been planning to walk down the aisle with another woman. If anyone had a right to question his judgment where it came to his relationship with women, he sure did.

Little wonder Charity had a few doubts, too.

"You don't have to feel guilty, you know. We're two consenting adults."

"I know." Her voice whispered across the patio as softly as the summer breeze.

He went to her, wrapped his arms around her and pulled her back against his chest. She was a perfect fit, and he nuzzled his lips to her neck. "This wasn't just a roll in the hay, cinnamon girl. I care about you."

She sighed, leaning back a little and tilting her head against his. "When Donnie comes back, I won't be able to... I mean..."

"You don't want him to catch you in my bed."

She nodded.

In spite of the twisting in his gut, Garrett understood. Being a mother came first with Charity, and that included setting a good example. Intellectually he had to admire that. It didn't do squat for his libido, however.

"At least that means we've got the rest of tonight and tomorrow morning," he said.

Half turning in his arms, she lifted her face to his, her expression so sweet and troubled he ached to ease her concerns.

"Yes," she said simply, and kissed him.

No determined pass rusher on any football field had ever brought him so swiftly and thoroughly to his knees.

Chapter Ten

The workers on the assembly line glanced in Charity's direction as she toured the chocolate factory with Garrett. She could see the questions in their eyes.

Is she sleeping with the boss's son? Is that how she got the catalog job?

With an effort, she resisted the temptation to check for a scarlet *A*—or some modern equivalent—pinned to her blouse.

Huge vats of melted chocolate combined with nuts and fruits poured their contents into molds that then wound their way on conveyor belts through a cooler and to the wrapping machines. The workers, mostly gloved women with their hair covered by white shower caps, inspected the candy bars, discarding those that didn't meet quality standards.

The truth was, Charity hadn't made love with Garrett for almost twenty-four hours, since Donnie had returned home yesterday. Already she missed the intimacy she'd shared with Garrett and desperately wished she was free to go to his bed morning, noon and night, unconcerned that her son might discover her.

Or that her conscience would raise its insistent voice.

She'd stolen one night. She should be satisfied with that.

She wasn't.

"Mostly our Christmas line features Santa Clauses, angels, chocolate trains loaded with toys, that sort of thing."

Charity had to forcefully drag her thoughts back to the job at hand and what Garrett was saying. She leaned toward him to be heard over the roar of the equipment.

"I need some samples to photograph," she told him. "I'll set the shots up at home. If you don't have any objection, I think it would be good to have some pictures of the workers, too. Give the consumers the idea that the Fun House Candy Company is all one big happy family."

"Sounds like a good idea. I can arrange that." His hand heated the small of her back as he ushered her safely around the end of a conveyor line, his gentle touch sending an electric jolt of yearning sizzling right down to her toes. "Having their pictures taken will be the highlight of their whole career for most of these women."

"Pretty boring job, huh?"

"It drove me crazy the one summer I worked here. Hell of a good motivator to find myself a different career." He held open the door that led to a second assembly area. "Besides, I'm allergic to chocolate."

She halted midstride. "Are you serious?"

"Hives. One bite and I have to buy out the entire supply of calamine lotion at Grazer Drugs."

"Guess that means you're not in charge of product tasting," she said with a laugh. What irony the man who would inherit the company couldn't enjoy the product. And what a relief Donnie wasn't allergic, too, which would have been another guilty arrow pointing to Garrett's paternity.

There were fewer people working in this area, and one entire assembly line was shut down. Screwdriver in hand, Bud was bending over a control panel. Glancing up, he spotted Garrett and Charity in the room. He shoved the screwdriver into his overflowing tool belt and came in their direction.

"Somebody ought to be talkin' to your dad about the overdue maintenance on all these lines," Bud said without preamble. "The ball bearings are worn thin, and half the V-belts are frayed. We're gonna have a major shutdown one of these days if somethin' isn't done soon."

Garrett was surprised Bud would approach him with the problem. They weren't exactly on cordial terms these days, though they'd both tried to be civil when Hailey and Charity were around.

"That's Harry Baumgarten's job," Garrett said. "He's the factory manager. Why don't you talk to him?" Garrett sure didn't know anything about the inner workings of the plant and didn't really want to know the details.

"I have. Every time I talk to him, he says he's going to do something about scheduling the deferred maintenance but nothing ever happens. Tell you the truth, I think he keeps forgetting."

"Isn't Mr. Baumgarten way past retirement age?" Charity asked.

"He doesn't want to quit." Bud pulled a rag from

his hip pocket and cleaned his hands. "Says if he retires, he'll die. I think since his wife passed away several years ago, the factory is all he's got left. They never had any kids."

"I'll talk to him about the problem," Garrett promised. Baumgarten had been old when Garrett had worked in the factory, or so it had seemed to him as an adolescent. Now the man had to be well over seventy and had probably been with the company for close to fifty years. Hard to throw a man out on his ear after that much dedication, but if he wasn't doing his job...

"Look, I've done what I can to keep the machinery rolling, and I can't exactly go over Baumgarten's head to your father about this," Bud said. "But if the maintenance schedule isn't sped up, you're in for real serious problems when we get to peak production this fall."

"I'll take care of it," Garrett repeated.

Bud glanced from Garrett to Charity. "Everything okay with you and Donnie?"

"We're fine. I've got my darkroom all set up now."

"That's good, sis. Stay in touch, huh?"

"I will."

"Well, gotta get back to work."

He left, and Charity said, "Bud must be terribly worried to bring up the maintenance problems to you."

"It wouldn't be that he's trying to get some extra overtime to support his new wife? Or make waves just before Dad goes into labor negotiations with the union?"

"Bud isn't like that." Charity's eyes flashed as

she leaped to her brother's defense. "He loves machinery of any kind, whether he owns it or someone else does. He claims he can actually hear a well-tuned machine singing to him. If he says there's a problem, there is. And probably one that's too serious for him to fix himself."

Someday Garrett would like to see that fierce love and loyalty in Charity's eyes and have it meant for him. But he wasn't all that sure how he could earn it.

They repeated the tour of the plant, this time with Charity checking the light and taking a few shots to develop at home. She was all business.

In contrast, Garrett's thoughts were out of sync with hers, wondering how he could seduce her back into his bed.

He was still developing a strategy to do just that when she barricaded herself in the darkroom later that afternoon.

"When the red light's on, nobody can go inside," Donnie explained. "She gets real, *real* mad if you do."

Garrett hooked his hand over the boy's shoulder. "Well, I sure don't want your mom mad at me. How 'bout we play some catch?" A little exercise might help to get Garrett's mind out of the very determined rut it was in.

Donnie brightened immediately. He'd been looking bored since they'd picked him up from the park recreation program that morning.

"I'll get my mitt," he said. "And my bat, too."

He thundered up the stairs to his room and back down again in a flash, making Garrett wonder how somebody who weighed about sixty pounds could make so much noise when he ran.

The street was empty of life. A couple of cars were parked along the curb, but the occupants of the stately Victorian houses were either at work or hiding behind closed doors. Like Charity was hiding from Garrett, he suspected.

He and Donnie tossed the ball back and forth a few times, Donnie's arm strong and his throws accurate for such a little kid. Whoever his father was, the guy was missing out on something really special, watching his son grow and mature.

Garrett frowned. The thought that *he* might be the one who'd been missing out was disquieting. Surely Charity wouldn't have denied him—or any man—the privilege of seeing his son grow up.

"You want to try hitting some?" he asked the boy.

"Yeah! Sure." Grinning, he dropped his mitt and picked up the bat, taking a couple of practice swings. "Bet I can hit a home run."

"Okay, get ready." Garrett tossed the ball overhand.

Donnie took a big swing—and missed. He went running down the street after the ball, catching up to it when it rolled to a stop in the gutter. He came trudging back up the block and threw the ball to Garrett.

"How 'bout we use the wall for a backstop?" Garrett suggested.

Rearranging themselves crosswise of the street, Garrett threw another pitch. This time Donnie topped it, and the ball dribbled about ten feet into the street.

"That's getting a piece of it, son. Next time try to keep your swing level."

He took a practice swipe with the bat. "Did you ever play baseball, Garrett?"

"A little when I was a kid. But I liked football better."

"Mom said she 'n' Uncle Bud used to play baseball in the vacant lot down the street."

"Bet she was good." That would also explain how she'd managed to bean the shotgun-toting gangsters with a film canister at Kate Bingham's wedding, he thought with a smile.

"But soccer's still the best." Spreading his stance, the kid looked like a major-league hitter getting ready for a three-two pitch.

Garrett grinned, imagining Donnie's father—whoever he was—probably loved sports, too.

The next pitch was right in there. Donnie's swing connected with a satisfying *tink* of the metal bat. The ball soared over Garrett's head. He watched it sail right through the front window of the neighbor's house. The sound of glass shattering disturbed the peaceful neighborhood.

Garrett grimaced.

"Oh, man," Donnie groaned. "Mom's really gonna be mad at me."

"It's okay, son. My fault for having you hit that direction." First thing—after he retrieved the ball from the neighbor's living room—Garrett was going to buy the boy a backstop. No wonder there weren't any other kids playing on the block, assuming any lived nearby. The whole street felt like an old-folks' home.

CHARITY WAS in the darkroom when she heard the phone ring. She expected Garrett to pick up. When it kept on ringing, she got worried, almost as if the tone itself was a warning that something was wrong.

She reached the phone on the tenth ring.

"Sis, is that you?"

"What's wrong, Bud?"

"Hailey called. She's coming unglued. Those darn teenagers got into the pig parlor and attached the water hose to a keg of beer. Rambo drank himself senseless."

"Don't those boys have anything better to do with their time?"

"I guess not. But now Hailey doesn't know what to do. With all the problems we've got here at the plant, I can't get away."

Charity shot a glance toward the darkroom and her unfinished work, and wondered briefly where Donnie and Garrett had gone.

"Okay, I'll go out there," she told her brother. Though mostly Rambo took his own sweet time about sobering up. But she could understand why Hailey, a town girl, would be concerned. Sounded like she needed a little hand-holding.

Outside, she discovered Garrett and Donnie. When she explained what was happening, they both volunteered to come with her.

"I've never seen a drunken pig before." Garrett canted her a wicked grin as he got into the passenger's seat of her Chevy. "How could I pass up a chance like this?"

Before they reached Main Street, she'd figured out why both of them had been so eager to escape the neighborhood.

"I didn't mean to break the window," Donnie assured her after she'd heard their confession.

"It was a heck of a hit," Garrett said. "I had no idea he could send one out of the ballpark like that."

She rolled her eyes. "The park is exactly where you both should have been. That street's too narrow for a decent game of baseball."

Donnie scrunched down in the back seat. "I'm sorry, Mom."

"Mrs. Buckworthy got a little hysterical about broken glass all over her living room, but I calmed her down. I gathered she's not used to kids playing in the neighborhood."

"Or grown-ups, either, I imagine."

"I told her to go ahead and have the window fixed. I'd pay for it."

"No, you won't. Donnie did the damage. He'll pay."

"Mo...om! I don't have any money. I'm just a little kid."

She suppressed a smile. Her son, who often protested he was getting too big to be kissed goodnight, was now using his youth as an excuse. "We'll work it out, son. You can do extra chores."

"Ah, gee..."

Garrett's hand rested on her thigh. The shock of his touch, so warm it heated through her denim skirt, nearly made her swerve off the road. All afternoon she'd been trying to avoid him—hiding in her darkroom.

"It was as much my fault as Donnie's," he said. "Why don't you let me pay?"

"Because Donnie needs to learn responsibility." Taking his hand, she moved it away from her thigh.

"It was a pretty big window. Expensive, I'd guess. Maybe a couple of hundred dollars."

Feeling slightly sick to her stomach, she made a quick mental inventory of her checking account. "All right, if you insist." She shot him a glance. "You can pay ninety percent."

The deep, booming roll of his laughter spread over her like a warm blanket on a cold winter night. He was a hard man not to like, even more difficult to keep at a distance. Ever since his botched marriage to Hailey, he'd insinuated himself into every facet of her life, both waking and sleeping. And now they'd been lovers. Again.

If he pressed, even a little, she doubted she'd be able to keep her vow to stay out of his bed when Donnie was in the house. And yet she knew whatever decision she made would only be temporary. Early this morning, she'd heard him talking on the phone to his agent.

He'd leave Grazer's Corners—the sooner the better from his perspective. And she'd be left behind.

Almost as soon as she'd come to a stop in front of the Arden farmhouse, Donnie blasted out of the car. It was like he'd been gone for years and couldn't wait to get back to his old familiar stomping grounds.

With equal speed, Hailey appeared on the front porch. Garrett lingered near the car.

"Oh, I'm so glad you've come," she cried, hurrying down the steps. "I was gone for a while and I didn't know the boys had been here. And then I found Rambo. I thought he'd died. I didn't know what to do so I—"

"It's okay, Hailey." Hugging her sister-in-law, Charity tried to calm the young woman.

"I feel just awful. I mean, there's nothing I do around the farm that's right. I wanted so much to please Bud, and all I do is mess up. I even got sick to my stomach trying to help him take care of some new little pigs."

"I don't think Bud cares if you're the best hog farmer in the world. He loves you. For him, that's enough."

Struggling to calm herself, Hailey smiled weakly. She looked over Charity's shoulder at Garrett, who was standing beside the car. "Thanks for coming. I know you didn't have to—"

"Relax, Hailey." He tucked his fingertips into his jeans pockets, pulling the fabric taut across his pelvis. "There're no hard feelings on my part."

Charity wondered again that Hailey had chosen Bud over a man like Garrett. In her view, however much she might love her brother, there was no comparison between the two men.

They found Rambo pretty well passed out in the barnyard. He opened one blurry eye as they approached, grunted a miserable-sounding *groonk* and closed it again. He looked like he had the grandmother of all headaches.

"Is there such a thing as AA for hogs?" Garrett asked.

"Not that I know of." She gave the animal a gentle pat on the snout. He didn't even budge, though he started to snore. "Donnie," she called. "Bring the hose around. We've got to cool Rambo off. Then we've got to get him into the shade. He'll get sunburned if we don't."

"Sunburned?" Garrett raised his brows.

"They have very sensitive skin, almost like humans."

"Apparently they don't have any more sense than humans do, at least not about overindulging." Garrett gave Rambo a tentative shove with his foot. "Don't tell me I'm supposed to move this ton of pork chops."

"I won't. But that's exactly what we have to do."

Getting Rambo on his feet was like getting any other thousand-pound drunk moving. Not easy.

Grunting as he lifted Rambo's rear end, Garrett said, "I'm gonna have a long talk with those kids. Assuming I can still walk tomorrow."

"You know where to find the youngsters who are doing this to us?" Charity asked.

"I've got a pretty damn good idea."

By the time they were through, they were all laughing and cursing—words unfit for Donnie's ears, but Charity didn't have the strength to worry about it. She rationalized he'd probably heard worse on the school yard or soccer field.

It troubled her, though, that Hailey seemed so at loose ends when she tried to help. Raised in the country-club set, she was definitely a fish out of water. Charity could only hope the learning curve would improve a little. She was sure Bud had intended that they remain on the farm and raise their family there. She wasn't so sure that would make Hailey happy, however determined she might be to please her new husband.

Garrett, on the other hand, wasn't at all uncomfortable with farm chores. And he, too, was a part of that same country-club set. Choking back a giggle, she supposed she ought to give him credit for having expanded his horizons.

IT WAS AFTER DINNER when Garrett finally had a chance to catch Charity alone. She'd gone back into her darkroom—he was beginning to think of it as her *cave*—right after they'd cleaned up the kitchen. He'd waited impatiently, and the instant the red light switched off, he was inside with her, pulling the door closed behind him and turning the light back on. The interior glowed in the muted light, the scent of freshly poured chemicals pungent.

"What are you doing?" she gasped, her eyes wide with surprise.

"I'm going crazy, that's what I'm doing. Rolling in the hay with a drunken hog is not how I want to spend my time with you."

He hauled her into his arms and silenced her startled objection with his mouth. For just an instant, she resisted, then melted into his arms, parting her lips for him. He reveled in her taste, the sweet, honeyed warmth of her. The heat that had been simmering in him all day rose to the boiling point, scorching him where her breasts pillowed against his chest.

He ran his hands over her back, splaying them across the swell of her hips, pulling her hard against his arousal.

She made a soft mewling sound, her tongue partnering with his, her fingers kneading the muscles of his back.

Blood pounded through his veins, and his breathing was harsh.

"Aw, cinnamon girl..." He lifted her blouse and

cupped her breast. His thumb flicked over lace and nylon, pebbling her nipple, the weight of her breast soft and pliant in his palm.

She groaned softly. "We can't...Donnie..."

"He won't come in, not with the red light on."

Garrett was afraid she might push him away, but she stayed with him, feathering kisses along his jaw, teasing at his lips. As hungry and eager as he.

"He might need me...."

"He'll call or knock." Garrett was the one who needed her now.

He rocked her into the nest of his hips, pressing her more tightly against him, angling her body so she could feel him in that sensitive V between her legs.

"Oh..."

Her sweet sigh of pleasure aroused him with masculine pride. There was no way she could deny she wanted him. He hadn't meant to take her here in the darkroom—had just wanted a kiss, had wanted to convince her to come to his bed later that night—but he could feel himself reaching the brink of control. No other woman had ever brought him to a fever pitch so quickly. None.

But he couldn't—

Suddenly her hands were on the snap of his jeans. It snicked open, and the zipper slid down, releasing him.

"Charity, you can't mean—"

"Hurry, Garrett. Please." Her whispered plea promised the moon and stars, heaven. "I've wanted this all day. Wanted you."

"Aw, baby..." No man would have the willpower to resist that invitation. Garrett didn't try.

Catching her around the waist, he lifted her, balancing her on the edge of the counter, hip high. Her panties, no more than a wisp of fabric, ripped as he pulled them from beneath her skirt. Her sandals dropped to the floor with a plop.

Her kisses rained down on his face. "This is crazy," she sobbed. "I can't stop."

He swallowed her muted cries with a deeper kiss, then lifted her again, inserting himself into her hot, honeyed sheath. A shudder went through her, and she went very still. Slowly he pressed. Her legs wrapped around him. He thrust again, harder, deeper, straining to keep himself in check, to give her all the pleasure she deserved. He slipped his hand between them, stroking her.

Her head lolled back, baring the tender column of her neck to his view. Her breath came in quick little pants.

The glow from the overhead light made everything seem surreal, the most erotic dream Garrett had ever imagined. But she was real. And he drove into her again.

Her release tightened around him, pumping, drawing everything he had from his body. He clamped his mouth shut to stifle the shout of joy that threatened to erupt.

"Oh, my..." she sighed. Her head dropped to his shoulder. "Nothing ought to feel that good."

"Yeah." He kissed the damp beads of perspiration that sheened her forehead. "After Donnie goes to bed tonight, come to my room. Or let me come to yours."

She trembled in his arms. "Yes, I'll come."

He held her a moment longer, then moved back and helped her down from the counter.

"Hey, Mom!" Donnie pounded on the door. "You gonna be done in there pretty soon?"

Garrett met her gaze, and his lips hitched up. "Perfect timing," he murmured.

Even in the red light, he could see her blush deepen. Shaking her head, she called to her son. "I'll be right there, sweetheart. Just give me a minute."

Chapter Eleven

Charity cuddled against the hard, masculine body next to her. Inhaling, she caught the scent of musk and sex, his and hers. Dimly she realized she'd have to get up soon and go to her own bed. But her body was still limp with exhaustion from Garrett's love-making. Even after the quick release of their desire in the darkroom, one more time had not been enough. She'd come eagerly to his bed later in the evening. Talk about a man with endurance!

She grinned sleepily and stretched, feeling the pleasant tenderness between her legs. Come to think of it, she'd kept up with him pretty darn good, if she did say so herself. And she'd never imagined she would do anything like she had in the darkroom. She wouldn't be able to step into the place without remembering...and blushing.

"Mom! Come quick!"

She bolted upright in bed, her eyes blinking, her heart beating like an out-of-balance threshing machine. She shoved her hair back from her face.

It wasn't night at all. The morning sun streamed in through the window—*Garrett's* bedroom window. He was there next to her, his hair mussed, a sheet barely covering the lower half of his naked body.

Not even that much covered hers.

''Oh, my God...'' What would Donnie think if he found her here?

Scrambling off the bed, she snatched up the robe she'd dropped to the floor last night and tugged it on. Her nightgown was nowhere in sight. She wasn't at all sure exactly when or where she'd shed that. Not that it mattered now.

''What's wrong?'' Mumbling, Garrett shifted on the bed and the sheet settled even lower.

''For heaven's sake, cover yourself up,'' she hissed, shoving her feet into her terry slippers. ''Donnie could come in here any second.''

Yawning, he stretched. ''Why would he wanna do that?''

Charity clamped her teeth together. The man was impossible. Didn't he realize—?

''Mom? Where are you?''

Mortified to have been caught, she wrapped the ties of her robe and hurried to the door, yanking it open.

Her son was standing right there, wide-eyed, his cheeks flushed, wearing cotton pajamas, so innocent it nearly broke her heart. Would he now be disillusioned by her wanton behavior?

She swallowed hard. ''Good morning, sweetheart. What seems to be the problem?'' The smile she forced felt like a rubber band that had lost its elasticity.

''It's Rambo, Mom. He's in the backyard. I heard him snorting and honking—''

''In Garrett's backyard?''

"Yeah. I looked outside and I think he's making a real mess. I hope Garrett's not gonna be too mad."

"What don't you want me to be mad about?"

Charity's head snapped around. Garrett had appeared in the bedroom doorway, and he was wearing only briefs—blue ones. Oh, damn! Couldn't he have at least pulled on some jeans?

"It's Rambo." Donnie grabbed his idol's hand, trying to tug him down the hallway. "I don't know how he got here, but he's making a real mess. It isn't my fault. Honest, it isn't."

"I know that, sport."

"Wait! Don't you dare go outside dressed like that, Garrett Keeley." Good grief! What would people think? "Put some pants on."

"Anything you say, ma'am." His grin was positively sinful as he went back into the bedroom and returned a moment later with his jeans.

She blew out a relieved sigh.

At least Donnie hadn't questioned why she'd come out of Garrett's room first thing in the morning with hardly a stitch of clothes on. Obviously she wasn't cut out for the role of lover. She had too many other responsibilities, to her son and to her pig farm. Just look what had happened without her there to oversee the place. Clearly someone had left a gate open, allowing Rambo to get out of the yard. She doubted it had been Bud.

THE BACKYARD vegetable garden, planted by the prior owner of the house, was in shambles. Rambo had neatly rooted through a row of young carrots, devoured the better part of a spring asparagus crop and was now taste-testing the green onions. From the looks of things, his rapid recovery from his hangover had given him a ravenous appetite, as well as the urge to travel.

"Phew, Mom. Rambo stinks of onions." Donnie sat astride the hog, tugging at his ears to get him to leave the garden. He wasn't having much luck.

Rambo objected to his mistreatment with a *wronk* and kept right on eating.

"Get him out of there, son."

Doing his best, Donnie kicked his heels into the hog's ribs. Since he was barefoot and couldn't get a lot of leverage around the bulk of the animal, Rambo didn't even notice.

"Don't worry about it," Garrett said, appearing to enjoy the whole ridiculous scene. "Looks to me like the crop is a total loss."

"I'm sorry, Garrett."

He slid his arm around her waist. She'd taken time to pull on jeans and a top, but Garrett's half-dressed, bronzed, muscular body made him look like Adonis in the long rays of morning light, though she might have hoped he'd bothered to close the top snap on his jeans. Nonetheless—or maybe because of his casual ease with his own body—she wished she had her camera with her. He'd make a wonderful study in masculine beauty, perfect for a living-art class. Except she didn't like the idea of any other woman ogling him, fellow artist or not.

"Come on," she said, "let's see if we can get that animal under control. Do you have a rope?"

"There might be something we can use in the garage, maybe a clothesline." Still with his arm around her, Garrett sidestepped them away from Rambo's path. "Based on what we saw yesterday, and now your hog getting loose, I'm not sure Hailey's going to make it as a farmer's wife."

Oinking contentedly in spite of Donnie's continued efforts to play cowboy on his back, Rambo started on a row of radishes.

"Of course she is," Charity said in her sister-in-law's defense, though she had a fair share of doubts herself. "Hailey's an Arden now. She'll get the hang of things. She just needs a little time."

Garrett tucked a strand of her unkempt hair behind her ear, sending a shiver of awareness down her spine. There was tenderness in his eyes and memories of the night they'd shared. There was something else, too, which Charity couldn't quite identify.

"I'd say family was the most important thing in the world to you," he said softly. "And you're already including Hailey in that protective circle of yours."

"We Ardens have always had to stick together. Gramps used to say that made us strong." But it hadn't made Charity's mother strong; she'd vowed to do better.

"I envy you." With the sun haloing his blond hair—and a thousand pounds of hog rooting in his garden—Garrett lowered his head to kiss her.

"Well, I never!"

They both jumped at the haughty, well-cultured voice of the neighbor, Mrs. Buckworthy. Charity instantly recognized the formidable woman from the photos she'd taken of the local garden club for the *Grazer Gazette*—and was just as quickly mortified to have been caught kissing a half-naked Garrett in his backyard first thing in the morning.

"I want to know the meaning of having a pig...a carnivorous *pig* in this neighborhood." Mrs. Buckworthy carried gardening gloves, wore a straw hat and had a decidedly angry scowl on her face.

"He's a hog and he only eats vegetable matter, ma'am," Charity said.

The older woman granted Charity a briefly scathing look before addressing Garrett. "Yesterday I had my window broken, young man, and today my garden has been decimated by this...this *creature.*" She gestured dismissively toward Rambo. "I don't know what the Realtor told you, but we have zoning laws in this town. We won't stand idly by and see our neighborhood turned into a barnyard...or a daycare center and worse." She shot both Donnie and Charity an insulting look.

Garrett began in a soothing tone. "Mrs. Buckworthy, I'm sure we can—"

"My son has as much right to be here as you do, Mrs. Buckworthy." Bristling, Charity interrupted, not nearly as ready to mollify the woman as Garrett.

Mrs. Buckworthy's eyebrows rose infinitesimally, communicating more disdain and disapproval in that single gesture than she could have said in a thousand words. "We are not accustomed to unwed couples in the neighborhood *shacking up* together." She whispered the accusing euphemism as though the mere thought offended her.

Charity's face flamed a bright red, and for a moment Garrett thought he was going to have to physically restrain her from attacking the old biddy. Instead, Charity turned away with great dignity, her chin held high, her back straight, and simply went about the business of herding the wayward pig out of the garden. Her restraint was something to behold, and Garrett knew it had cost her plenty.

"Mrs. Buckworthy, I think it's time you leave." Taking her arm, he escorted her toward the open gate. "I'll be more than happy to pay for your losses, but I don't want you to set foot on my property ever again."

"Really, young man," she huffed. "You simply don't understand. You come from a good family, and your father would sorely disapprove of all these goings-on. That woman simply isn't suitable—"

"I think she is *quite* suitable." If Charity could so quickly leap to Hailey's defense, Garrett could damn well return the favor. And she *was* suitable—to be in his house, in his bed and in his... "I think you ought to keep your opinions to yourself, if you know what's good for you."

Mrs. Buckworthy sputtered and fussed, finally shaking off his grip when they reached the sidewalk. "You'll be hearing from my attorney, Mr. Keeley."

"Fine by me." Distractedly he watched the woman stride across the street to her old Victorian house with its neat lawn and shrubs, and a flower garden that Rambo had methodically divested of anything that bloomed. No wonder she was upset. But Garrett's primary concern was with Charity.

Just what did he expect of her, want from her? What did he really think she was *suited* for?

Great sex didn't begin to cover it.

But he was still hoping to land a spot on an NFL team before the season started. In spite of how she'd been treated by Mrs. Buckworthy, he doubted Charity would be all that eager to leave Grazer's Corners. She seemed wedded to the town, to her family's history here and their legacy—a subsistence farm with little more than a great view. He suspected, given a choice, she'd jump at the chance to move back to that hardscrabble farm. And despite Charity's defense of her new sister-in-law, he was convinced Hailey wouldn't last long as a farmer's wife. Unlike Charity, she simply didn't have the stamina and guts for the job.

Realizing he was standing on the sidewalk looking like he'd just rolled out of bed, he retreated into the house to finish dressing.

No woman had ever affected him the way Charity did. But given the fiasco with Hailey, how could he judge for sure how he felt about her? He couldn't make a commitment. And that's exactly what she deserved—a man who knew to a certainty that he loved her and would devote the rest of his life to making her—and her son—happy.

He might never be that confident of his feelings.

Maybe he didn't have enough emotional depth to feel that strongly about anyone.

That stunning thought nearly sucked the wind from him. If that was the case, he ought to keep the hell away from her because he'd bring her nothing but grief. She was too vulnerable, too loving to be treated in the same casual way he'd dealt with most of the women in his life.

And that might be all he was capable of handling.

CHARITY DROPPED to her knees and looped a rope she'd found in the garage around Rambo's neck. It was all she could do to breathe. She swallowed convulsively. She would not disintegrate beneath the whip of Mrs. Buckworthy's abuse, would not let her get the upper hand. Raised on the wrong side of the tracks, she'd been insulted before and with far more vindictiveness.

But never in front of Garrett.

Shame knotted in her belly as she pulled the rope tight. How could she have thought she could live with herself if she moved in with Garrett? If they became lovers?

"Mom, I think Rambo misses us. That's how come he followed us to Garrett's house."

"You may be right, Donnie." She'd heard of dogs and cats traveling great distances to follow their masters, but never a *hog!*

Rambo nuzzled Donnie's hand, and the boy petted his snout, the mutual affection between the child and his pet obvious. "I kinda miss him, too."

"I know, honey." Odd how torn she felt, missing the farm as much as Donnie did but wanting to be with Garrett, too. Clearly her ability to reason had slipped away, probably somewhere in the darkroom.

"Seems like us Ardens get in trouble when we come to town. Breakin' windows 'n' stuff," Donnie said.

Forcing a smile, she tousled her boy's curly hair and tried to tamp down the sting of emotions. She hadn't wanted Donnie to suffer the verbal slings and arrows of townspeople who thought raising hogs was a lowly occupation. "Guess they can take the Ardens off the farm, but they can't get the farm out of the Ardens."

"Huh?"

"Never mind, honey. It's just an expression." Another reminder that she didn't belong here, not in town and not with Garrett. "Help me get this beast tied to something sturdy till I can get Bud to bring his truck into town." Her chin trembled. Then maybe they should all pack up and go home.

Garrett might be used to shacking up with a woman—he'd certainly had enough women in his life to know the rules and not be troubled by criticism. But Charity wasn't nearly as comfortable with the idea as she'd hoped. For her, it simply wasn't working.

For a moment, she felt herself floundering, untethered from any place she could call her own. Living with the newlyweds had been awkward at best; staying with Garrett now seemed impossible. Where, she wondered, did she belong?

"Need any more help there?" Garrett came sauntering out of the back door dressed in jeans, a T-shirt with the sleeves ripped out and running shoes.

In spite of herself, Charity's gaze dropped to the snaps on his jeans and the fly that was nearly white from wear. Images of him above her, loving her, his body sun-bronzed and naked, popped into her mind unbidden. Blinking, she tried not to think about that.

"I think I've got things under control for now," she said, though she couldn't seem to hog-tie her thoughts as easily as she had lassoed Rambo. "I'll call Bud to bring the truck into town and haul Rambo back home."

"I'll ride back home with him," Donnie volunteered. "He doesn't like to be in the truck all alone."

"How 'bout you go put some clothes on, Donnie. I'd like to talk to your mom."

"'kay." Giving Rambo one last scratch between the ears, Donnie ran off toward the house.

Garrett hooked his thumbs in his pockets, framing his hips and drawing Charity's attention to his pelvis once again. He was such a big man....

"I'm sorry about Mrs. Buckworthy," Garrett began. "She was way off base."

Standing, Charity brushed the dirt from her knees and tried to look anywhere but at the denim that was stretching between his hips. "I can't blame her, Garrett. If Rambo got into her garden—"

"It's her other comment that was out of line. You didn't deserve that."

"Maybe I did." Pursing her lips, she expelled a long breath and finally met his troubled gaze. "A woman who moves in with a man is fair game."

"That's ridiculous. Thousands of women live with—"

"Need I remind you, Grazer's Corners is a very small town. The rules are different here than they would be in a big city, and if you break them...well, there's a price you have to pay. I thought I'd be able to live with that. I can't, not when my son is likely to suffer, too."

His forehead furrowed, deep creases that suggested he really did care. "Does that mean you're moving out?"

"I think it would be better for all concerned. Maybe I can still find an apartment somewhere." Heart aching, she lifted her shoulders. "Or maybe I can talk to Bud again about not being quite so lovey-dovey with Hailey."

He clasped her upper arms with his big strong hands, his thumbs circling the curve of her shoulders. "I don't want you to go, Charity."

Her heart leaped, and she waited for him to add

a reason for her to stay, something about love and happily-ever-after. Something about not ever wanting any other woman. Something about spending their lives together and growing old in each other's arms.

But the words didn't come.

Mentally she lifted her chin another notch. "I'd better go call Bud so we can take care of the immediate problem. I wouldn't want Mrs. Buckworthy calling the zoning cops on you. Then I'll try to sort through the rest of it." And do what she knew she had to do, whatever else her heart might be telling her.

He dropped his hands to his sides. "I was going to go find those kids who got Rambo drunk and give 'em a good talking to this morning, but I'll stick around till Bud comes."

"No, I'd rather have you come down on the kids." And in truth, she needed a little time alone to rein in her wildly vacillating emotions. "If you can stop them, that'd be a big help. They need to understand giving an animal alcohol isn't a joke. It could seriously harm Rambo."

"You're sure you don't need me here? Wrestling that many pork chops all at once won't be easy."

She shrugged. "Bud and I have managed before. We'll be okay." The two of them had been forced to take over the farmwork years ago. They'd been a team while Garrett had been earning his fame and fortune in a much different arena, and living a lifestyle where Charity would never feel at home.

GARRETT found the town jocks exactly where he expected them.

The football practice field hadn't changed much. There were a few more initials carved into the old wooden goal posts, and the grass looked a bit scruffy and unkempt, but outside of that everything was pretty much the same. Even the rickety bleachers where he'd kissed his first girl looked unchanged.

For a moment, Garrett was swept with a powerful sense of nostalgia. He'd trained hard on this field and learned a lot about life from Coach Riddler in the process. Mostly the memories were good, the coach's influence on him a more positive force than that of his own father.

With a shake of his head, he refocused on the present.

In the center of the field, two kids were doing stretching exercises; another couple of jocks were jogging around the oval track going so slowly they probably weren't even breaking a sweat.

"Is that as fast as you clowns can go?" he called to the runners. "I've seen five-year-olds doing better. And they were girls!"

Both heads turned in Garrett's direction, and there was a flash of challenge in the boys' eyes before recognition set in.

"Hey, Keeley!"

"How's it going, man?"

Nonchalantly Garrett crossed the field toward them. "I'm looking for somebody to help me out."

"Hey, man, whatever you need."

The two boys who'd been stretching ambled over to see what was happening, giving Garrett a loose-limbed, one-of-the-guys salute. All the guys wore running shorts and tacky gray T-shirts shorn to midriff length. The joggers were sweating more than they should have been, suggesting they weren't exactly in peak condition. But that's how it often was in preseason. Coach Riddler would whip them into shape when the time came.

"I've got this friend," Garrett said, letting his gaze shift among the adolescents. "Understand me now, she's a real good friend. Seems she owns a pig farm out east of town. Kind of a run-down place, but she really likes it there." A bit of guilty color began to darken the cheeks of the two kids who'd been running. "She's especially fond of an old hog she calls Rambo."

The taller youngster darted a quick look at his buddy. His friend had found something fascinating to study on the toe of his running shoe.

"I'd take it as a personal favor," Garrett continued, "if everybody would sort of watch out for that load of pork chops—and the nice lady who owns him—and not let anything bad happen to either one of them. If you know what I mean. Think you can help me out with that?"

"Yeah, sure, Mr. Keeley," one of the kids who'd been stretching said.

Garrett didn't think that boy or his friend had had anything to do with the beer incident, so he zeroed in on the other two. "How 'bout you guys? Think you can handle that?"

The taller one shrugged. "Guess so."

When the second one didn't respond, Garrett moved in close enough to smell the kid's sweat. "How 'bout you, son?"

"Hey, man, I don't even like pigs. I'm not going out there for nothing no more, okay?"

"That suits me just fine, thanks. Now, then—"

Garrett rolled his shoulders and stretched the kinks out of his neck "—I thought I'd run a few laps this morning. You guys think you can keep up?"

Without waiting for an answer, Garrett jogged off the grass onto the track. The kids fell into step beside him. Fortunately his knee was feeling pretty good, so after a half lap he picked up the pace. Breathing a little harder, the youngsters stayed with him as Garrett knew they would. Nothing like the challenge of trying to keep up with a pro to motivate a young person. Garrett had sure felt that way when he first hit training camp, not wanting anyone to outshine him—and every season it almost killed him to stay with the others.

As he finished the first lap, he said, "How you guys doing? Anybody want to make a race of it?"

Only one of the youngsters was even able to grunt an affirmative response.

With an ease that pleased him—not because he was beating a couple kids but because it meant his leg was on the mend—Garrett accelerated so fast the kids were left several yards behind him. He rounded the end of the track with his legs and lungs pumping hard, and feeling damn good about himself. When he got back home, he was going to call his agent. He was ready to go back to work, the sooner the better.

He crossed the spot where they'd started, cruised through another lap, then slowed to a jog. The boys straggled up beside him, all of them panting hard and sweat dripping down their faces.

"You did good, men. You hung in even when it hurt." He slapped their shoulders and gave the youngsters who'd done the mischief at the Arden farm an extra high five. They got the message—he could outrun and outmuscle them, but he didn't hold a grudge. They wouldn't be lugging any more beer kegs around unless it was to a party of their own. And if he were their coach, he'd see to it that didn't happen, either.

After telling them goodbye, he stopped for a drink from the faucet, running the water long enough that it cooled to lukewarm.

He was anxious to get back to Charity, to convince her to stay with him. But if he succeeded, would that be fair to her? he wondered. And what about Donnie?

"MOM, CAN I RIDE my skateboard while I wait for Uncle Bud?"

"Of course, honey, but stay on the sidewalk and wear your helmet. And please don't get into any more trouble with Mrs. Buckworthy."

"I won't, Mom. I promise."

Smiling into the mirror, Charity wondered if it was possible for any little boy to actually keep that kind of a promise. Men, it seemed, were virtual magnets for trouble.

She brushed her hair, pulling it back and looping it in a loose knot. Bud had said he had to finish his chores and it would take him about an hour to get here to pick up Rambo. Garrett would be back soon, too. And Charity hadn't decided yet what she should do.

Every instinct she had screamed at her to run away. She'd already risked too much by moving in with Garrett. However much he might want her in his bed, he didn't love her. If he did, he would have said something. He wasn't exactly a bashful guy. But when the opportunity had come to speak up, the silence had been deafening.

Emotion tightened thick and hot in Charity's throat. She'd been lying to herself all along. She'd never wanted a "temporary" arrangement with Garrett. From the beginning, from that night at the lake, she'd wanted it all.

And had known damn well that wasn't in the cards.

She'd known that eight years ago. There was no reason why the shock of that truth would bring tears to her eyes now.

Through the blurring of her tears, she looked around the room trying to remember where she'd put her suitcase. A witch's cauldron of emotions churned in her stomach. Her head began to throb. She never should have moved in with Garrett. She had to leave.

Outside, she heard Rambo squeal. *Oooooo-eeeeennnnkk.*

She shot a look out the window and to the street below, catching the terrifying scene in the time it took to snap a camera. A scream formed in her throat.

"Donnie!"

Chapter Twelve

Garrett turned the corner onto his street and slammed on the brakes.

"Oh, my God..."

Rambo was galloping wildly down the street, squealing and screaming. Behind him, his ankle snared by the rope that was tied around the pig's neck, Donnie was being dragged along the asphalt.

Garrett jammed the gearshift into Park, threw open the door and raced toward the pair of them.

On the playing field, there'd been times when he'd thrown an interception and he'd had to sacrifice his body as the last man who could make the tackle to save a touchdown. This time it was even more important that he make the play. Donnie's life was at stake.

He launched himself at the animal, colliding full force with a thousand pounds of flesh and bone. His shoulder took the brunt of the impact with the pig, and his knee collided with the street. Pain exploded up his thigh. He ignored everything except wrestling the animal to a halt.

He heard a woman screaming, assumed it must be Charity, but he was too busy wrapping his wrist and hand around the rope to keep Rambo from blasting off again. The crazed hog must have been scared out of his wits or he wouldn't have been dragging the boy down the street. But somebody else would have to release Donnie. It was all Garrett could do to hang on to the animal.

Once he calmed Rambo, he checked what was happening to the boy. A few feet behind him, Charity was cradling her son in her arms, his head in her lap, his plastic helmet looking almost too big for the youngster.

Above her, Mrs. Buckworthy was armed with a broom and a fearful, guilty look. She'd been the one, Garrett knew, who had frightened Rambo into fleeing down the street.

"Things like this didn't happen in our neighborhood until that Keeley person moved in and brought you...you farm people into town," the old biddy cried. "Football players! That's not a fit career—"

"That football player just saved his son's life! If you have any compassion at all, Mrs. Buckworthy, you'd go call 911. My son—" Her sob swallowed the rest of her words as she caressed Donnie's face. Tears tracked down her cheeks.

Immobilized by surprise and shock, Garrett clung desperately to Rambo to keep him from bolting again.

His son?

He'd wondered. He'd even thought it was possible. But he'd never really believed she would keep her son's paternity a secret from the boy's own father.

Until now.

THE SCENT OF LEMON room freshener hung heavily in the air like a citrus orchard, not quite covering the antiseptic smell that was so much a part of every hospital. Charity looked almost as pale as Donnie had when they'd brought him into the emergency room. Since the doctor had shooed them out of the examining room, she'd been pacing, not able to rest for a minute. And Garrett didn't dare sit down for fear his knee would stiffen up on him and he wouldn't be able to walk at all. The damn thing was throbbing like crazy.

Meanwhile he had a million questions. No, he mentally corrected, just one question that really mattered. *Was he Donnie's father?*

If the answer was yes, then there'd be a whole raft of other questions, all of which would have to wait until they knew about Donnie's condition.

God, he didn't know what to think. A son? A boy he'd only just met? He'd missed seeing his first steps and hadn't had any of that middle-of-the-night business with a crying infant. What about the kid's first day of school? He should have been there.

If Donnie was his son.

That football player just saved his *son's life.* Had that been only a slip of the tongue?

Why the hell would Charity keep a secret like that from him? It didn't make any sense.

Father unknown the birth records had shown. But Charity knew. She had to.

She turned from looking out the window, from watching cars arrive and depart, patients being wheeled out, visitors bringing flowers. Her beautiful brown eyes, normally deep and luminous, were red and puffy from crying. She looked so vulnerable a band tightened around Garrett's chest and he ached to hold her.

But his own emotions were bouncing all over the place, and he couldn't seem to take that last step that separated them.

Why hadn't she told him the truth?

"What's taking so long?" she asked, pleading for an answer he didn't have.

"These things take time." The platitude didn't work for him, either, but he didn't know what else to say.

Is it my son in there? Dear God, he wanted to know. Yet the possibility scared him to death. He might lose his boy before he'd ever had a chance to really get to know him.

If that happened, he'd damn well string Mrs. Buckworthy up by her thumbs—and personally turn Rambo into a thousand pounds of pork chops.

Every time he closed his eyes, the scene replayed through his mind. He'd rather face a whole army of linebackers than go through that again, the fear that he wouldn't be able to stop Rambo's runaway stampede before it was too late.

Charity's chin trembled; tears pooled in her eyes, threatening to overflow. "He looked so little on the gurney. What if he needs me and they won't let me...?" A single tear spilled down her cheek.

That wrenching emotion broke his paralysis.

He opened his arms, and she stepped into his embrace. A shudder shivered through her body. She didn't sob, but he could feel the dampness of her tears seeping through the front of his shirt. He could tell how hard she was working at being strong. She was like that, tough on the outside but with a soft heart that was capable of giving more love in a minute than he'd experienced in his whole life.

Had they made a baby that night? Was Donnie his son? Why hadn't she told him?

The questions echoed one after the other in his mind, tolling like the chant of angry fans in a crowded stadium.

God, please don't let Donnie die.

"I feel so helpless," he murmured, holding her tight. "What can I do to help you?" *To help* our *son.*

"Just hold me."

He smoothed her flyaway curls back from her face, kneaded her scalp with his fingertips. And wondered.

"Mr. and Mrs. Arden? I'm Dr. Keith."

The doctor wore green surgical scrubs and looked to be only a little older than the high-school boys Garrett had been jogging with that morning. Or maybe the man's youth was a reflection of how much Garrett had aged in the past few hours.

"How is he? How's Donnie?" Charity asked, and neither of them bothered to correct the doctor's assumption that Garrett was Mr. Arden—his patient's father.

"He's a very lucky little boy, Mrs. Arden. Though he has a mild concussion, the helmet saved him from a far more serious injury. Other than that, he has a sprained ankle and a lot of abrasions and contusions. By tomorrow he'll be just fine. Children are amazingly resilient."

Charity nearly collapsed with a relief so sharp it left her breathless. The adrenaline that had been keeping her upright drained away, and she felt faint.

Only Garrett's arm around her, his strength, kept her upright. That and her need to be with her son.

"May I see him?" she asked.

"Of course, but only for a moment. I'd like him to rest for a while, as a precautionary measure, you understand. Then you can take him home."

In a blur, Charity followed the doctor down the hallway. She was vaguely aware of nurses moving about, doctors being paged over the loudspeaker and Garrett walking beside her. Garrett's hand on her arm, steadying her. Garrett, Donnie's father, the man who had saved her son's life.

He was limping because of what he'd done and wincing with every step; his jeans were ripped at the knee. His act of courage, determination and brute strength might well have cost him his career. She owed him so much....

The shock of seeing Donnie looking so tiny and fragile in that huge bed, his head wrapped in a bandage, nearly brought her to her knees.

"My baby..." She feathered his face with kisses, stroked his pale cheek with the back of her hand. Her heart filled her throat when his eyes blinked open.

"Mom? My head hurts."

"I know, sweetheart. It'll feel better soon."

"Rambo—it wasn't his fault. Mrs. Buckworthy scared him, and the rope got—"

"Shh, sweetheart. It's all right. Rambo's fine, and you will be, too. Sleep now and then we'll go home." Back to the farm, back where they belonged.

The guilt of having put Donnie at risk lodged in her chest.

Leaning past her, Garrett rested his hand on Donnie's shoulder. "Rest now, son, and later I'll let you beat me at checkers again."

A tiny, heartbreaking smile fluttered around the corners of Donnie's sweet mouth. "You're easy to beat. Gramps taught me good."

"Yeah, well, maybe I just have to practice harder."

To Charity's surprise, she heard emotion choking Garrett's words. Had he heard that slip of her tongue, her admission of the truth in an instant of sheer panic?

They waited until Donnie drifted off to sleep, and then they stepped into the hallway. Charity leaned her head back against the wall, emptying her lungs of all her fear and fright with a deep sigh.

"I need to know, Charity, and I want a straight answer."

She looked into his eyes, saw that he'd heard the truth, and her tongue felt as thick as a cow's.

"If I'm his father, I have a right to know, dammit. Don't hold out on me any longer."

He'd saved his son's life. He deserved the answer. But dear heaven, the truth could cost Charity and her whole family the farm they'd sacrificed so much to save.

"Yes," she whispered.

Like a videotape playing in fast forward, myriad emotions sparked in his eyes—elation, pride, pleasure, all mixing with residual confusion.

"Why didn't you ever tell me? I had a right—"

"You can't tell anyone, either. Please, Garrett, I promised. No one can ever know. No one." Most particularly Garrett's father.

His confusion darkened into something akin to anger and he narrowed his eyes. "Why the hell not? Why does it have to be such a deep, dark secret?"

"Don't ask, Garrett. It's just the way it has to be. In a little while, when Donnie wakes up, I'm going to take him home. To the farm. And I think it would be better if you didn't see him again."

"He's my son."

"He's *my* baby and *my* responsibility. If anyone asks, I will deny we ever had this conversation, I swear I will. Now, please, leave. Go home."

When she tried to turn away, he snared her by the arm, his fingers digging into her flesh. "That's not how it's gonna be, cinnamon girl." He was standing too close, his voice intimate and intimidating, a muscle flexing in his jaw. "We made a baby and now we've slept together again. I'm not going to let you walk away without giving me all the answers I need."

In a panic, she glanced up and down the hallway. They were alone, and he hadn't raised his voice. But the thought that someone might overhear their conversation sent a knife of fear cutting right to her heart.

"Come out to the farm tomorrow. After Bud goes to the factory. I'll send Hailey to the store or something, and Donnie will be resting, so we can be alone." Her mouth dry as toast, she darted a look at a passing orderly. "I'll tell you everything then, but you have to promise me you won't tell another soul."

With a slow shake of his head, he said, "You're going to have to explain why the secrecy is so important before I make a promise like that."

"Then I won't—"

"Yes, you will, Charity. Tomorrow you're going to tell me the truth. All of it."

GARRETT JUGGLED the phone on his shoulder while he tried to pull his pants on, the project complicated by the fact he could hardly put any weight at all on his bum knee. He'd had it iced all night, and the damn thing was still throbbing. Under other circumstances, the pain might have kept him awake. But he'd had other things on his mind that had been even more effective for producing insomnia.

A son! Damn, he could still hardly believe it.

"Tampa Bay is still thinking about picking you up, but it's not looking good," his agent said over the phone.

"They don't know what they're missing," Garrett mumbled under his breath. At the moment, the only thing they were missing was a gimpy, over-the-hill quarterback who wouldn't be able to run away from a two-legged elephant.

"Not to worry. I've been talking to a couple of Canadian teams—"

"Canada!" he exploded. "Hell, Tommy, I'm an NFL quarterback, not some second-rate—"

"Settle down, Garrett, and listen. What they do best in Canada is pass, and you do that better than any quarterback in either league, north or south. A season or two up there, and the NFL boys will be beggin' you to come back—at a premium, buddy. Trust me on this."

Standing storklike, he managed to get one leg into his pants. "I don't know, Tommy. I never thought I'd have to—"

"Hey, man, you don't have to make a decision right this minute. I'll float your name out there and see if anybody takes the bait. That'll be soon enough to see if they'll make it worth your while."

Garrett didn't much like the idea but he supposed he'd have to go along, at least for the moment. "Keep working on other teams for me, Tommy. Canada isn't exactly high on my list." And it would be a hell of a long way from Charity...and his son. God, he still couldn't quite get over the fact that he had a child. It was some kind of a miracle. The reverse of immaculate conception, he supposed, but he was darn excited about the prospect of being a father. A *real* father.

After he hung up with his agent, Garrett managed to finish dressing and hobbled out to the car. He was more than anxious to find out from Charity why she had to keep it such a deep, dark secret that he was Donnie's father.

Frankly, he thought with a grin, he'd like to shout it from the rooftops.

CHARITY SHOT A GLANCE at the clock over the sink. Nearly ten o'clock. That's when Garrett had said he'd be there to learn the truth, and Hailey was still fussing trying to clean up the mess she'd made while cooking last night's meat loaf. She hadn't even begun to start on the oven.

"Why don't you leave that?" Charity suggested, desperate to have her sister-in-law out of the house before Garrett arrived. Anxiety burned in her stomach like she'd swallowed a pound of hot Mexican chiles and then lit the concoction with a torch. "I'll take care of things."

Hailey took a scouring pad to the blackest loaf pan Charity had ever seen, then added a lot of elbow grease. Her usually carefully manicured nails were a mess, her fingers reddened by too many soakings in dishwater. "You have to look after Donnie. Poor baby. This will only take me a minute. And the one thing I'm getting good at," she said with a laugh, "is cleaning up burned-on messes."

"No, really, I'd rather you do the shopping." Stepping to the sink, Charity took the scrub brush from Hailey's hand. "You might even want to stop by to see your parents. You know, kind of take the morning off."

"Why is it I get the feeling you're trying to get rid of me?"

Guiltily Charity looked away.

"Okay, what gives? Bud and I have been worried about you. You moved out in a such a rush, then all of a sudden last night—"

"Please, Hailey."

"It's Garrett, isn't it? Did you have a fight with him?"

"No." Charity rinsed the loaf pan and set it on the counter to air dry. She certainly wouldn't call her admission of Garrett's paternity a fight, but he'd looked ready to do battle for the right to claim his son.

Eyeing her with a combination of curiosity and concern, Hailey dried her hands on a paper towel. "I've been thinking about getting a job in town. Maybe at Harmon's Department Store. Or I could find something to do in Modesto. That way Bud and I could have a place of our own and save up for a house. It'd take a while—"

"You'd leave the farm?" she gasped. "This is Bud's home."

"Charity, honey, I know you love this place. And so does Bud, I guess. But I...I feel so damn useless and it's like I've been stuck in Siberia."

"We're only five miles from town."

"To me it feels like a thousand. My friends never drop by. It takes forever just to go to town for a loaf of bread. I feel so isolated." With a toss of her head, she shifted her long blond hair behind her shoulder. "Mind you, Bud and I are only thinking about it right now. But if I can get a decent job..."

"Well, you'd better not try to take Betsy Muller's job at the department store selling makeup," Charity quipped, though she didn't feel a bit like making jokes. "Betsy's an institution in town." And had certainly had her eye on Moose Harmon, the store's owner, until he became engaged to Kate Bingham. Now that their wedding had been called off...

Charity swallowed hard. How could Bud possibly leave their home, the town they'd been such a part of, the place that had been their safe haven when their mother had given up all pretense of being a parent? There were memories here. Good times and a loving home with their grandparents and each other. Even when Charity had moved in with Garrett, she'd known she'd come back. It had only been a temporary arrangement, a brief time when she'd succumbed to temptation. She'd known it would end.

And being there with Garrett, loving him and trying to act like a townie had nearly cost her son his life.

"Okay, you don't have to talk to me if you don't

want to,'' Hailey said. ''I'll get out of your hair. But Bud and I do worry about you. More than anything else, we want you to be as happy as we are.''

The emotions were so thick in her throat, Charity found she could barely draw a decent breath. However much trouble Hailey was having becoming a farm wife, she was an Arden. She cared. But not about the pig farm or the land.

''Give me a couple of hours,'' Charity pleaded, the words rasping against the tension of her windpipe.

''Sure.'' Resting her hand against Charity's arm, she squeezed lightly. ''I'll be gone in a sec. Don't sweat that frying pan that I tried to cook the eggplant in. I'll buy you a new one.''

Hailey was as good as her word. Within five minutes, she'd gotten in her car and driven away.

With her gone and Donnie restricted to resting in his room, the house felt ominously quiet. She was going to have to face Garrett any moment now. Though she tried, no words came to her, no excuses he would understand, and guilt gnawed in her belly.

As she went to change from the clothes she'd worn to feed the pigs, she fleetingly wondered how a woman should dress to explain her actions to the father of her son, and then decided it didn't matter. She still had to protect her son's legacy. At the time of her decision, she'd seen no way out, no other choice. Now she didn't know what to think. Only that the truth could destroy all she held dear.

The sound of tires on the gravel driveway was as painful as fingernails on a blackboard. A firing squad wouldn't have been harder to face, the agony over much quicker.

Would he ever believe she'd done the only thing she could eight years ago? Or recognize how much it had cost her?

Chapter Thirteen

"How's Donnie?"

Instead of letting Garrett into the house, Charity opened the screen door and stepped out onto the front porch. The air was already warm with the threat of a summer heat wave, the birds silenced by the rising temperature.

"The doctor was right. Children are amazingly resilient." In contrast, Charity had been an emotional wreck. Whenever she'd dozed off last night, thoughts of this moment had startled her awake like a bad dream coming true. "I've told him to stay in bed, but he's already getting restless."

"Should we take him in to see the doctor? Maybe there's something—"

"Really, he seems fine. It's just that his back was all scraped, and when he rolls over…" The lump that had been in her throat since the accident nearly cut off her air. "It could have been so much worse. If you hadn't been there…"

Placing his hand at her nape, he kneaded the tense muscles of her neck. She knew she ought to move away. Making a full confession wasn't going to be easy, and the difficulty would be compounded if she was distracted by how good it felt to have him touching her.

With a force of will, she walked to the edge of the porch and sat down on the steps.

"You can't put it off forever, Charity."

She lifted her head to look up at him and squinted at the bright sky that formed a backdrop of blue around his head. The sun glanced off his hair like it was a field of ripe wheat. She drew a lungful of air, warm and scented with his fragrance and that of the nearby snapdragons and roses, then exhaled slowly.

"After that night at the lake, I was terribly embarrassed by what I'd done. That's why I didn't return your phone calls. I didn't think I'd be able to face you. It was more than a month later when I realized..." Still wanting to deny the truth, she broke off her story.

"You were pregnant," he finished for her with an insistent tone. "Go on."

"I wasn't paying any attention to the calendar. Pretty stupid of me, particularly considering I was having trouble keeping my breakfast down. I thought I had some kind of a flu. And then Gramps had his stroke."

Garrett hunkered down next to her on the top step. "You must have been scared out of your wits."

"I was. I was terrified Gramps might die, and I didn't want to tell anyone I was going to have a baby, not right then. It would have just added to Grandma's worries."

He hesitated a moment as though he hated to give voice to his thoughts. "You could have gotten rid of the baby."

She gazed at him levelly, knowing exactly what

he was asking. "I never even gave that a thought." She hadn't wanted to be pregnant, but after the shock had worn off, she'd wanted his baby. More than he would ever fully understand.

With the back of his hand, he smoothed a few flyaway strands of hair from her face. She hadn't braided it yet that morning, and it hung loosely about her shoulders.

"Thank you," he said softly.

His expression of gratitude eased her fears more than anything else he could have said or done. At least he didn't hate her for carrying his baby to term, for loving and raising his child. Perhaps he wouldn't even be angry to know that all this time she'd harbored a secret—that she'd loved not only his child but Garrett, as well.

"I didn't know how to reach you, or really if you'd want anything to do with me. Or the baby." Pursing her lips, she remembered how much courage she'd needed to take that next step. "I went to your house to ask for your address, thinking I'd write to you at school and tell you what had happened. Your father—"

"You talked to my father?" His eyes widened in stunned disbelief.

"He was the one who answered the door. I think that was when your mother was so ill."

"She had chemo that fall. I wanted to stay home, but Dad insisted I go back to school and play out my senior season. He wanted me to get the Heisman so bad he could taste it." He shifted his position to sit on the step beside her. When he stretched out his leg, he rubbed his knee, and Charity wondered if he'd reinjured it saving Donnie. "Mother died that next spring."

"Yes, I heard. I'm sorry."

He acknowledged her sympathy with a nod. "Are you telling me Dad knew you were going to have my baby?"

"He didn't know then. And I certainly didn't tell him. When I showed up he recognized me, of course, and just sort of laughed at me." Hugging herself, she shivered at the dreadful memory. Even if he hadn't known about her pregnancy, Douglas Keeley made it quite clear she wasn't a suitable candidate for the mother of his grandchild. Or even to be seen with his son. "He said I was the third or fourth girl who'd been looking for you and that you must have had a hell of a good time that summer. That I'd have to get in line."

Garrett swore under his breath. "Why'd he tell you a stupid thing like that?"

"You mean it wasn't true?"

He had the good grace to flush slightly. "Well, I might have been sowing a few wild oats during the summer, I admit. But it wasn't as bad as all that. And it still doesn't explain why you had to keep it a secret that I'd gotten you pregnant. Did you really think I'd turn my back on you and not take some responsibility for what had happened?"

"I didn't know what to think at that point. The whole house was in a turmoil because of Gramps. Then we had two cases of TB among the pigs. We had to destroy the entire herd. On top of the huge loan Gramps had taken out to modernize the farm, we were going to lose everything. Then your father came to see me."

"My father came here? Why, for God's sake?"

"Apparently he'd heard I was pregnant and he was afraid I would name you the father and ruin your football career."

"Why would he think that? I sure wouldn't have been the first jock to get some girl pregnant by mistake."

She winced but knew he was right. He certainly hadn't intended to get her pregnant. "Your father seemed to think I was going to force you to marry me. I wouldn't have done that, Garrett. I swear I wouldn't."

He speared his fingers through his hair, sending the waves into disarray. "He should have told me, dammit! It was my decision to make, not his. If you'd only written me, I would have—"

"I couldn't write you. Not after I agreed to your father's proposition."

His head whipped around, his eyes blazing. "Dad propositioned you?"

"Not like that." She laid a calming hand on sun-warmed denim and felt the muscles of his thigh tense beneath her palm. "He offered me enough money to pay off our bank loan and establish new breeding stock. The catch was, I had to swear I'd never, ever tell *anyone* that you were my baby's father. Including you."

"My dad bought you off? My God..." He shot to his feet; his hands clenched into fists as if he wanted to hit someone. "And you went along with that? How the hell could you?"

"I didn't have any other choice, Garrett." His anger propelled her to her feet, too, prepared to defend her decision whether he liked it or not. "If I hadn't agreed to your father's plan, we all would have been thrown out in the street. Gramps was so sick he could barely talk and was bedridden, Grandma was wearing herself to a nub taking care of him, Bud was still in school. The only possible way I could save the farm—and my grandparents' home—was to accept your father's offer. So that's what I did."

Garrett swore again, low and succinctly.

"And the fact is," she continued, "even now, if you so much as hint that you know you're Donnie's father, he can still take the farm away from us."

"No. You can't be serious."

"Seriously stupid, is probably more accurate. I convinced Grandma to sign a note to your father. He's threatened that if you ever learn the truth, he'll record the note, and foreclose if we can't pay it off—which I assure you, we can't, even though I save every penny I can. And the farm will be his."

"He'd foreclose on his own grandson? I don't believe—"

"You can believe anything you want because you don't have anything to lose. I do."

"I've already lost seven years of my son's life. I'm not about to miss another minute if I don't have to. And I want my son to know he has a father."

"Oh, my God, Garrett. I thought you'd understand." Panic sliced through her. "Because you saved his life, you had a right to know the truth. But you can't destroy the only home Donnie's ever known." Her home, too.

"I'm not going to destroy anything. I'm going to—"

"Hey, Mom, can I have some—?" The screen

door swung open, and Donnie stood there in his pajamas. "Hi, Garrett. Did you come to play checkers with me?"

"Go back inside, honey," Charity ordered quietly, though she was teetering on the edge of hysteria. She never should have told Garrett the truth. *Never!* And now she'd come close to inadvertently revealing the secret to her son, as well. "I'll be right there."

"I just wanted some orange juice. I can't get the lid open."

"I'll get you some in a minute." She met Garrett's gaze, silently pleading with him not to risk turning her son's life upside down. And her own.

Slowly Garrett pulled his gaze from Charity to Donnie. His son! Anger pulsed through his veins, and adrenaline spurted through his system, pumped there by Charity's revelations. His father had denied him the right to know his boy, a beautiful child who was a whiz at checkers and a damn fine soccer player. An athlete with lots of natural talent. The boy might not look anything like Garrett, but he'd managed to pass along a few of his genes.

Fury blurred his vision bloodred.

His father had interfered in his life before, demanding he excel at football, insisting he take an interest in a factory that he found far less compelling than a history book about the American Civil War.

But this was a giant step beyond simple interference.

Douglas Keeley had denied him something beyond measure. His son.

With his emotions so volatile, Garrett didn't think

he could manage a quiet game of checkers. Other things came first.

Under his breath, he asked Charity, "How big is the note?"

She paled, then told him an amount he understood she would find staggering on her income.

"Give me a rain check on the checkers game, son," he said. "I've got some things I have to do."

"Betcha you're afraid I can beat ya." Donnie grinned broadly, a smile Garrett now thought might be a lot like his own.

"I'll get you, kid. It may just take me a while." He turned to Charity. "I'll be back," he said, low and rough.

"Please, Garrett, don't—"

He didn't wait around to listen to her plea. He had a man to see.

He hoped to God his anger would simmer down before he got there. Because, at the moment, he wanted to punch the hell out of his own father.

HE DIDN'T BOTHER to greet Arabelle at the reception counter. That didn't stop her from calling out, "Congratulations, Garrett, I heard the good—"

Shoving through the security door, he went up the stairs, taking them two at a time. He walked past his father's secretary, only vaguely aware she'd said "Congratulations." The closed door to his father's office didn't slow Garrett down a bit. Hell, he would have knocked it off its hinges if the damn thing had been locked.

His father was alone, papers and spreadsheets strewed across his usually neat desk. He looked up, and a big smile crossed his face.

"For a new employee, you're a hard man to find, son. Tommy's been looking all over for you."

Garrett put on the mental brakes. "Tommy? What does my agent want?"

His father's grin broadened. "Orlando, son. They're picking you up as their first-stringer. They're ready to sign on the dotted line."

Momentarily distracted by the good news, Garrett let the possibilities sink in. Not a Canadian team but Orlando wanted him, an up-and-coming expansion franchise with enough backing to hire topflight players. Within five years—or less with the right quarterback—they'd be contenders. Skilled coaches. Young but talented players.

He hadn't been sure he'd actually get a second chance. But there it was, assuming his knee held up. He still could snatch that coveted Super Bowl ring.

For a moment, he allowed himself to imagine the luxury of showing off that ring and that brought him up short.

Show it off to whom? he wondered. His son lived in California, not Florida. And so did Charity.

His earlier anger seethed again and he focused on his father. "I'll call Tommy later. Right now I want to know why you didn't tell me about my *son.*"

Douglas Keeley's smile dissolved. He narrowed his eyes, and his lips tightened before he spoke. "I don't know what you're talking about."

"Charity told me, Dad."

"Has it occurred to you that woman might have been lying to you?"

"What about the loan you made to her? And your threat to foreclose if she told anybody the truth? Is that a lie, too?"

He paled slightly. ''What I did, I did to protect you, son. She'd come to the house once, looking for you, upsetting your mother, and I knew you wouldn't want—''

Garrett exploded with a string of epithets. ''What the hell gave you the right? He's my son, dammit!''

Under Garrett's verbal assault, Douglas shoved his chair back from the desk and stood. ''She would have ruined you. Wrecked your career before it even got started.''

''How? Because she was carrying my baby?'' Maybe he and Charity would have spent more time together; maybe Garrett would have been on the receiving end of all that love Charity had to give.

''I've never wanted you to know this, son. But the truth is, I was forced into marrying your mother. I'd gotten her pregnant...''

That stopped Garrett's fury as effectively as if he'd run head-on into a three-hundred-pound defensive tackle. ''Are you telling me you never loved Mother?''

''I tried. At first I even imagined I did. But dammit, if I hadn't had to marry her, I might have won the Heisman. I could have been a star in the NFL. Instead—'' he gestured vaguely around the office ''—I ended up running a damn candy factory like my father.''

Garrett stared at him stupidly. God, he'd never realized his parents hadn't loved each other, or that his father had resented him so much. No wonder Garrett had never figured out how to love someone else. No one had shown him.

Except Charity.

With a shake of his head, Douglas said, ''You

ought to be thanking me for getting rid of that woman so *you'd* have the chance I missed."

"You lied to me. You kept me in the dark about something I had a right to know."

"Dammit all! I kept you out of jail!" Douglas bellowed. "Give me some credit for that!"

"What are you talking about?" he asked tautly.

"My God, son. What were you thinking? The girl was only seventeen when you got her pregnant."

Garrett felt like he'd taken an unprotected punch to the gut. That night at the lake he hadn't been thinking about Charity's age, only about how he loved to see her smile and hear her laughter, how much he wanted to *make* love to her. Sure, he'd been filled with raging hormones, but he'd cared about her, too. He'd never intended it to be a one-night stand.

"If you weren't thinking," his father continued, "her brother certainly was, and he made the situation abundantly clear to me. And the risk I was taking with your future if I didn't step in to take care of matters."

"Bud? What the hell does Bud have to do with all the lying and secrets?" Garrett had understood from Charity that no one knew who was Donnie's father, not even her brother. She'd been sworn to total secrecy.

"He tried to blackmail me, the conniving, no-good pig farmer." A vein pulsed at Douglas's temple, and his face turned red. "How do you think he got his job here? And why do you think he's a rabble-rouser with that damn union of his? He hates me because of what you did to his sister."

Garrett's head spun. Charity's brother had known

who had gotten her pregnant and had used the information to blackmail his father? Garrett had never considered that bizarre twist. But it certainly explained the animosity between his father and the union steward—the whole Arden family, for that matter.

He clenched his fists and walked to the window, staring grimly toward the distant mountains, invisible in the haze of summer. Charity had had no part in the blackmail scheme. He was as sure of that as he was that the Sierra Mountains were hidden behind the curtain of dust and clouds.

"I had the impression Bud was a pretty good mechanic," Garrett said, "and knew more about the factory than anyone else in the company. I was even going to suggest he be promoted to factory manager when Harry Baumgarten retires."

"Over my dead body," Douglas muttered.

Garrett turned back to his father. "Have you noticed Harry forgetting things lately that he really ought to be keeping track of?"

"Maybe." He shrugged. "We're both getting old. And tired. Why do you think I wanted you to start learning the ropes around here? If you hadn't gotten this chance with Orlando… It's time for me to pass the reins to someone younger."

"Not to me, Dad. I'll sell pencils before I take over the factory. Since you've apparently hated the place all these years, maybe you can understand my feelings."

"But your office—"

"I wanted a way to hire Charity to do the catalog work." And so he could spend more time with her.

He'd never expected to discover her son was also his own flesh and blood.

"Now that you've got the chance to start over, you'd be a fool to get involved with her again. You should have married Hailey. She'd have made you a good—"

"I don't think so, Dad. And I want the note you're carrying on Charity's property torn up."

"That cost me a chunk of change, boy. Real money. The Ardens were heavy into debt. I can't just hand over—"

"I'll buy it from you, including all the interest she owes. I won't have that threat hanging over Charity's head any longer. Or my son's. And the whole town is going to know Donnie is mine and I'm damn proud of him." Though Garrett wondered if he'd ever be able to make it up to the boy that he hadn't been there for him all these years. He hadn't been there for Charity, either, he realized. She'd been the real victim in all of this, manipulated by both her brother and Garrett's father.

Amazingly she'd survived; in some ways, she'd even thrived. Garrett admired her for that. In fact, he *loved* Charity for her capacity to go on in spite of everything life dumped in her lap.

He wasn't sure, given the same challenges, if he could have done as well.

He hated to think how she'd react to learning her brother had instigated a blackmail scheme that forced Charity to live with the secret of Donnie's paternity. However large her capacity for love, she was bound to feel betrayed by what Bud had done.

The intercom buzzed, and Douglas jammed his finger on the button. "Marge, I want you to hold—"

"I'm sorry to interrupt, sir, but I thought you and Garrett would both want to know," his secretary said as smoothly as though her boss hadn't yelled at her. "Coach Riddler had a heart attack last night. He's in Community Hospital now. His condition is considered 'stable but guarded.'"

Garrett expelled a long breath and plowed his fingers through his hair. "Coach didn't look good when I saw him the other day," he said when his father turned back to him. "I should have guessed something was wrong."

"He's a good man. He'll pull through."

A whole generation of men, men who had influenced Garrett's life for good or bad, were aging fast. His father included, he now recognized, noting the deep grooves across Douglas's forehead and the tiredness in his pale eyes. When had his father gotten old? he wondered. Perhaps it had started when he was forced to marry a woman he didn't love.

And his mother had grown old, too, long before she had died, bitter with very little love to give her son.

What a tragedy. A trap Charity never would have slipped into.

Crossing the room, Garrett placed a hand on his father's shoulder. He might not ever get over his father making decisions about his life that should have been rightfully his own. But he also wasn't eager to break the tie to the man who had raised him.

"You'll like Donnie," he said quietly. "He's a terrific little kid. He can dribble a soccer ball like he was born to it and can beat the socks off of me at checkers. I hope some day you'll take the time to get to know him."

His father didn't respond. Garrett hadn't expected him to. The best he could hope was that Douglas Keeley would come around to his way of thinking later. If not, it was Douglas who would miss out...and Donnie, his grandson.

Soon Garrett would have to face Charity and tell her about Bud's involvement in this whole blackmail scheme. He didn't think telling her would be easy. But there'd already been too many secrets in Grazer's Corners.

He was determined to start fresh.

But where, he wasn't quite sure.

It was going to take a while to sort out his feelings and consider all of his options. *This time* he wanted to make damn sure he was doing the right thing—for everyone concerned.

Chapter Fourteen

It was like waiting for the other shoe to drop.

Three days since Garrett had learned he was Donnie's father. Except for a brief phone call from Garrett to Donnie, it had been three days of silence.

Charity ground her teeth. She wanted to scream. She wanted to cry. What in heaven's name was he thinking? What was he doing?

With a sigh of frustration, she refilled the feeding bins for the afternoon and bent down to pet Esmeralda. The sow's abdomen was so swollen with babies it had to hurt, and her breathing rate had begun to pick up. A new litter of pigs would be here soon, to tend and raise, earning the Arden farm a few dollars more than the cost of feed and supplies. A profit.

When Bud and Hailey moved out, she'd have to thin the herd. There was simply too much work for one person to handle. Then there'd be no profit at all.

Rambo trotted into the farrowing pen, nudging Charity's shoulder. *Wheenk,* he muttered impatiently.

"These things take time, Rambo. Esmeralda is

doing all the work. The least you could do is be encouraging.''

His ears perked up, and she gave him an affectionate scratch in his favorite spot. Maybe fathers had a right to be anxious, too.

Where was Garrett? Had he decided being a father didn't suit him after all?

Had he decided *she* didn't suit him, either?

The tears that had been threatening for three days crowded in her throat, but she refused to give in to them. Nor would her pride allow her to make a call herself. Garrett knew where to find her.

Coming to her feet with a determined shove, she hefted the wheelbarrow. She would *not* wallow in self-pity. Garrett had his own life to lead. So did she.

The fact that she loved him, and always had, didn't change that one whit.

At the sound of Bud's truck on the driveway, Rambo ambled in that direction, no doubt eager to let the other man in the family know he was about to be a father. Again.

''How's Esmeralda?'' Bud asked when he reached the pig parlor. He was wearing his blue mechanic's overalls, the thighs and pockets streaked with stains that no amount of laundering could remove.

''Ask Rambo. He's been checking on her hourly.''

Bud's experienced gaze swept over Esmeralda in an unconcerned way. ''Guess you heard about Garrett.''

Her heart seized, missing a full beat before starting up again. ''Has something happened to him?''

"He got picked up by the Orlando team. Their quarterback went down with an injury, and they made Garrett an offer. From what I hear, he took the next plane out."

For a moment, the world spun dizzily. Her stomach repeated the motion, and her hand covered her mouth.

Florida. Had he called Donnie from there? Three thousand miles from Grazer's Corners.

"I'm sorry, sis. I thought you'd want to know."

She nodded mutely. Of course she wanted to know. Garrett should have been the one to tell her. Obviously he hadn't thought about that. Not that it would have changed anything.

Garrett was gone.

Her knees turned all rubbery, and she sank onto the low wall of a juvenile pen. The newly weaned shoats came running, eager for a handout or a pet behind the ears. Charity gave them neither. Suddenly all of her strength, along with the hopes she'd secretly harbored, vanished.

"Sis, are you all right?"

"It's what he wanted. A new team." Her voice was flat, her mouth desert dry.

Awkwardly Bud tried to console her with a pat on her back. What she wanted was to be in Garrett's arms. But that wasn't going to happen. Ever.

"You want me to finish up here?" he asked.

"I have to pick up Donnie from Shaun's house pretty soon." Her son. Hers alone.

He reached for the shovel just as Rambo snorted at a new car in the driveway.

Shading her eyes with her hand, Charity watched a flashy red sports car pull to a stop behind Bud's battered panel truck, all the more incongruous because it was Garrett's car. *He was supposed to be in Florida.*

She stood. With an iron grip, she kept her emotions in check. He'd come to tell her goodbye; she was sure of it. She appreciated his gesture. Would wish him well. And then it would be over. In time, the pain would stop.

He had the swagger of a champion, that confident stride that said *Don't mess with me.* Dressed in an expensive sport shirt and slacks, he didn't fit in here at the farm any better than his car did. Nor did she and her son fit into his world.

"Thought you were in Orlando," Bud commented.

"I was."

"Yeah, well..." Bud lifted the wheelbarrow. "I'll leave you two alone—"

"No, what I have to tell Charity involves you, Bud. Stick around." His wasn't a pleasant request but an order.

Charity's gaze darted between the two men. She read simmering anger in Garrett's eyes, confusion in Bud's. "What's going on?" she asked.

"You want to tell her about your blackmail scheme, Bud? Or shall I?"

Bud's tanned cheeks deepened a shade. "I've never blackmailed anybody in my life, and you damn well know it."

"Wait just one minute," Charity protested.

Garrett ignored her. "How long have you known I was Donnie's father? Tell her that, Bud."

She gasped. "You knew? All this time—"

"I guessed, sis. I was at the picnic that night at

the lake. I saw you go off with him. Maybe I should have stopped you, but I didn't think—''

''Besides, you were hitting on Hailey,'' Garrett reminded him. ''Pretty distracting, wasn't she?''

''Look, you two. What's past is over and done with.''

''It isn't done with because Bud went to my father after you saw him and threatened to land me in jail.''

''I never did any such thing. Your old man got in a stew. I wasn't about to cry rape. Dammit, I knew Charity was mooning over you. She was in love with you even then, you sucker. But you were too busy chasing anything that wore skirts to give her the time of day. Or to take responsibility for—''

''For what I didn't know about? How could I? If you were such a damn good brother, why didn't you come to me? I would have taken care of Charity.''

The two of them were practically nose to nose, and Charity stepped between them. ''Don't you two big macho males dare leave me out of the conversation. This is about me. And my son—''

''*Our* son,'' Garrett corrected.

She shot him a withering glance, then turned to her brother. ''I want to know exactly what happened with Mr. Keeley, Bud. Exactly what you told him. And I want to know right now.''

''Charity, it's been a long time....''

''*Now,* Bud.''

He shrugged and jammed his hands in his overall pockets. ''We were in such trouble, with the farm and Gramps so sick. I couldn't see any way out. And hell, Garrett was a college jock. What kind of help could he be? But his old man—''

"You actually asked Mr. Keeley for money? For me?"

"For you and the baby. I figured a few hundred bucks a month would at least help out till I got a raise or two."

"Dad said you blackmailed him into hiring you."

"That's a lie. I'd already talked to the foreman and Harry Baumgarten. The paperwork had already been signed for me to start as a mechanic's helper when the school quarter ended."

"Did my dad know that?"

"Hell, I don't know."

"But the money, Bud. The loan to pay off the remodeling expenses. Did you ask Mr. Keeley for that?"

"Not exactly. When I mentioned you were only seventeen, he got his shorts all in a knot and went off the deep end. He jumped to the conclusion I was going to turn Garrett in but I never would have done that. I swear I wouldn't. He was so ticked off, he threw me out of the office. Later, when you came up with the money, I figured he'd developed a conscience so I let it slide."

Let it slide? Charity's stomach churned. So many misunderstandings. So many secrets. Bud had had no idea what she'd had to sacrifice to earn that money. He hadn't seen the agreement she'd signed, hadn't been aware of the vow she'd made to never reveal the truth. He'd only known about the money. And had been relieved.

She looked up at Garrett, into his familiar eyes, specks of gold glinting in the sunlight, and she was afraid to guess what she was reading there. "I never would have signed a complaint or testified against you. What we did, I wanted as much as you did."

He ran his fingertips along her hairline, dipping them slightly at her widow's peak. "I know that, cinnamon girl," he said softly. "But Dad didn't."

She tried twice before she could swallow the lump in her throat. "Is he going to call in the note?"

"It's been taken care of."

Her eyes widened. "What do you mean?"

From his hip pocket, he produced several folded sheets of paper she instantly recognized as the note she'd urged her grandmother to sign so long ago and her own promissory note for something far more valuable than money. "You can burn these or feed them to the pigs. You don't owe Dad a dime."

"You paid off the loan?" she asked, though she had little doubt that was exactly what he had done.

He glanced at Bud. "I might have been a broke college kid when I got Charity pregnant, but I'm not now."

"I've saved up some money," she said quickly. "I was going to start making payments. I can pay you back. It might take a little time." Just another twenty years or so.

"There's no need, Charity. I owe you that much and more."

"Look, guys, you don't need me here," Bud said.

Turning to her brother, Charity said, "All those years you knew it was Garrett, but you never once let on to me. Why?"

"I figured if you wanted me to know you'd tell me. I was trying to respect your privacy, sis."

Should she thank him for that? At this point, she didn't know. Eight years ago, he'd been as scared and unsure of himself as she had been. She understood he'd tried to help the family, not betray her.

"If you knew about Garrett, why on earth did you kidnap him, bring him here and shackle us together? Didn't it occur to you that the situation would be more than awkward?"

"Well, I had to take him someplace." With the toe of his work boot, he rearranged the pebbles on the walkway. "Hell, I'd stolen his bride right out from under his nose, hadn't I? I thought you and he'd, you know, that you would—"

"That I'd be the perfect consolation prize? You were matchmaking?" She nearly screamed the accusation. "Is that what you're saying?"

"Naw, sis, that's not what I—"

Mortified by what Bud had done, and how she had quickly and easily fallen into the trap, Charity began shaking uncontrollably. She hugged herself, but her teeth started chattering, in spite of the warmth of the summer day. Inside she was cold. So very cold and alone.

She didn't know whom to turn to. Bud had, at the very least, deceived her; Garrett had turned his back on her, flying off to Florida without a word of explanation virtually the moment she'd told him the truth about Donnie. Paying off the mortgage might be no more than a grand gesture motivated by guilt.

"*Now* you can give us some time together, Bud," Garrett ordered, his voice low and taut.

Bud shot him a look, started to say something, then thought better of it. He turned, picked up the wheelbarrow and headed for the barn.

Garrett tried to draw Charity to him, to console

her, just to hold her, to try to tell her how he felt, but she shrugged away from him.

"So, I understand congratulations are in order," she said with what sounded like forced brightness. The stubborn tilt of her chin, combined with her quavery voice, told him she was fighting for control. She had more guts than a wide receiver who went up for a ball knowing damn well he was going to get creamed whether or not he made the catch.

"How's that?" he asked cautiously.

"Orlando made you an offer, right?"

For a soccer mom, she seemed to know a lot about football. "I went down to talk with the coaches. That's where I've been for the last couple of days, doing red-eye flights. We're still negotiating."

"They'll put enough money on the table, I'm sure. It's your big chance. What you wanted."

"It's a long way from California."

"Give the man an A for geography."

Her uncharacteristic sarcasm gave him a jolt. She was hurting, he realized. Betrayed by her brother, deserted by him—as unknowing as he'd been. The woman had a right to a world of pain. She'd damn well earned it.

"Given training schedules and the regular season, going with Orlando would mean I'd only be in California three or four months a year."

She reached behind her neck to pull her long braid to the front of her shoulder, a gesture he'd observed many times. Mostly when she was nervous. And what he really wanted to do was loosen that hair, run his fingers through the strands and make love to her as he never had before.

"If you still want to develop a relationship with Donnie," she said, "I'm sure he'll be glad to see you whenever you're in town."

Garrett wanted more than to get to know his son. He wanted...

Hell, he'd been to Florida and back again, and he still didn't know what to do. He wished to God Charity would help him out a little here. A man who'd blown one marriage only weeks ago couldn't exactly trust his judgment now.

"So when do you think we ought to tell Donnie?" he asked.

Her gaze darted away from him, first to the weeping willow tree with branches that brushed against the house and then to the pig parlor. "He's not home now. He's at Shaun's."

"You want to pick a time?"

"I need a chance to talk to him first."

"Okay. Will you call me?"

Nodding, she pursed her lips.

He could stand up to a nine-man rush and stay in the pocket long enough to get off a pass so accurate it would go through a bull's-eye a foot across. But he didn't know how to deal with Charity's calm, cool demeanor. He wanted her hot in his arms, in his bed. That was definitely not the message that was coming across.

Never in his life had he felt so vulnerable. So unguarded. He was about to make a huge decision that would affect his whole future. Yet he couldn't seem to focus. His thoughts were all tangled up with Charity...and their son.

Hell, he was a quarterback. He was supposed to

call the plays. Instead, he felt like a bumbling water boy.

"Okay," he said finally. "I'm going to go see if they'll let me in to visit Coach Riddler now. Call me later."

She jerked a nod, then turned to walk away. Her back was ramrod straight, her hips barely swaying, her feet clopping along in big black boots. She was the most sensual, earthy woman he'd ever known in his life.

And he wanted her.

GARRETT TOOK county roads south of town to Grazer Community Hospital, passing farms marked with old houses and rows of ragged eucalyptus trees used as windbreaks. Small herds of cattle munched lazily on summer-dry grass or stood in the shade of an occasional sprawling live oak. In a plowed field, a tractor kicked up a line of dust that hung immobile in the windless air.

Garrett had liked living in the city. The excitement had worked for him—night spots, beautiful women, a chance to dissipate residual adrenaline after a big game.

As a young man, he'd been eager to get away from the slow pace of Grazer's Corners. Now it struck him as a good place to raise a kid. The town had decent schools, and youngsters had plenty of open space to mess around in where the worst mischief they could do was getting a hog soused on a keg of beer. There was little crime—assuming you ignored the odd shotgun-toting bandits who had disrupted Kate Bingham's wedding and the biker who had snatched Jordan Grazer from the church steps a week later.

With a wry smile, Garrett realized there'd been a real run on weddings that were better off for not having taken place. His included.

He pulled into the lot at the back of the hospital and parked. Inside he checked at the information desk, then made his way to Coach Riddler's room. He paused momentarily at the door, preparing himself to see his old mentor.

Coach looked up as Garrett entered the room and grinned. Assorted floral bouquets were squeezed together on the bed table and more were crowded on a wall shelf, filling the room with the scent of an overgrown garden.

"I hope you didn't bring any more flowers," the coach said. "This place is beginning to look like a funeral parlor."

"Guess I forgot." He clasped Riddler's hand, the older man's grip strong and firm, and Garrett felt a great surge of relief. Though the coach appeared to have aged years in the week since Garrett last saw him and looked like he'd spent too much time in a pool hall, he wasn't about to give up the ship anytime soon.

"Heard you got an offer from Orlando."

"News travels fast." Garrett pulled up the chair and sat down next to the bed.

"In Grazer's Corners? Can't spit without somebody hearing the news before it hits the sidewalk."

Garrett agreed with that assessment, particularly if Agatha Flintstone got hold of the news. "I would have been here sooner except I had to fly to Orlando."

"And?" Riddler persisted.

"We're still negotiating." And Garrett was still trying to make up his mind about his future.

Riddler passed his palm over the top of his head, smoothing his thinning hair, and frowned. "I must be worse off than I thought if they sent you around to cheer me up. You look like you just threw an interception that cost you a Super Bowl ring. What's wrong, son?"

Resting his elbows on his thighs, Garrett laced his fingers together, studying his thumbnail.

"Woman trouble?" Coach guessed.

"Yeah, you could say that." In the past, Coach Riddler had been there to listen to Garrett's dreams and ambitions, and bolster him during those dark moments of doubt. Garrett realized the reason he'd come today to visit Riddler was as much a cry for the man's help and wisdom as a gesture of friendship.

So Garrett told Riddler about Charity, and how he'd just discovered he had a son. Pacing the room, watching the sun dip lower in the afternoon sky, he related his bizarre kidnapping and his father's betrayal. He left out some of the intimate details about his relationship with Charity, but Coach got the picture.

"I know Charity Arden from the photos she takes for the school annual," Coach said when Garrett finished his story. "Fine young woman."

"Better than that. She's a survivor, as determined as any person I've ever met. Hell of a good mother, too." And so hot in bed, Garrett trembled whenever he thought of them together.

"Are you in love with her?"

Jamming his hands in his pockets, Garrett looked out the window. The monitor attached to Riddler's chest beeped with reassuring regularity.

"Three weeks ago, I was going to marry another woman. Now I can hardly remember her name, much less conjure up a very clear image of her. How the hell can I trust my feelings about Charity?"

"Your feelings are damn obvious to me. You're tied in knots and you can't seem to think straight. I'd say you love the girl."

Garrett glanced back over his shoulder to his coach. "She's real attached to Grazer's Corners. I doubt she'd be thrilled at the prospect of moving to Orlando and I'm not so sure I am, either. But I'll be damned if I'll stay here and work at the candy factory."

"You could coach football at Grazer High," Riddler said quietly.

Garrett did a mental double take. "You've been Grazer's coach for as long as I can remember. Once you're out of the hospital—"

"I figure this heart attack could be the best thing that ever happened to me. The missus and I are gonna get ourselves an RV and see some of the places we've talked about all these years. It's time for us to smell the roses." He gestured toward all the flowers in the room. "This is about as close as I'd like to come to a funeral parlor for a lot of years."

"I don't know, Coach. I'd never thought about—"

"I'm going to retire, son. I'd like nothing better than to turn over the reins to someone like you, who I know would do a good job, not only by winning games for the school, but by teaching boys to be men, too.''

That was a compliment hard to refuse and a responsibility that would weigh heavily on a man. ''I don't have a teaching credential.''

''You've got a degree plus enough credits in history to teach that subject along with coaching football. The kids all idolize you, and I'd say you have an in with the school board, your dad being a member and all. An emergency credential is easy enough to get, assuming you're interested.''

Was he interested? Or should he make one last try for the golden NFL ring?

When he'd worked out with the team in Orlando, he'd felt old and rusty. One hard shot to his knee, and his career was likely to come to an abrupt end. Then he wouldn't even be able to help Charity around the pig farm.

That thought brought him up short. He'd been thinking of them—he and Charity and their son—as a family. A *farm* family where there was love and laughter in the house, and a terrific woman in his bed. Making new babies. Lots of them.

Using the bed railing for leverage, Riddler shifted to his side. ''Sometimes a man has to trust his gut instincts to know what's right. Your instincts have always been pretty good, son. I'd go with them if I were you.''

Chapter Fifteen

Charity rummaged through a box of her old school papers and decided to chuck the whole thing in the plastic trash bag, one of several she'd already filled.

Since Garrett had left, she'd been in a frenzy of activity, cleaning the attic, making plans for the future.

A future without Garrett.

Stifling a sob, she lifted the flap on another cardboard box, peering through a sheen of unshed tears at Donnie's stored baby things. She picked up a crocheted crib blanket and hugged the softness to her, closing her eyes as the sweet memories poured over her. A single tear spilled, trickling down her cheek.

When she opened her eyes, a man was standing in the shadows at the top of the stairs to the attic.

Startled, she shrieked.

"Easy, Charity," Garrett said. "It's only me."

Her hammering heart slowed to its normal pace. "What on earth are you doing here?"

"More to the point, what the heck are you up to? This place looks like a cyclone hit it."

"If you must know, I'm doing a little housecleaning.'' Once and for all, she was going to put the past behind her.

He crossed the room, stopping in front of her. Idly he fingered the blue blanket she was using as a shield in front of her.

''Donnie's?'' he asked.

She nodded.

''Where is everybody? I gave a shout downstairs but nobody answered. If the attic stairs hadn't been pulled down, I never would have found you.''

''Hailey and Bud volunteered to take Donnie for ice cream.'' Charity had been grateful for the reprieve. She hadn't yet found the courage to tell Donnie that Garrett was his father—and in the next breath tell him that Garrett was leaving.

''Have you told him about me?''

''I thought you were going to call first, before you came over.''

''I'm not here to talk to the boy. I've come for you.''

''For me?'' she echoed.

Gently he took the blanket from her and tossed it into the box. ''I'm here to kidnap you.''

''Garrett, you can't—''

He silenced her by taking her hand and leading her to the stairway. ''It's a recent custom here in Grazer's Corners, I understand. Sort of a throwback to caveman days, I suppose. Or maybe it's the influence of all those Norman conquerors that Agatha Flintstone finds so fascinating.''

Awareness skittered through her, and she tamped down the image of being slung over Garrett's shoulder and hauled off to his secret lair.

''I can't go anywhere with you,'' she protested as

they walked down the stairs. "My hair's a mess, and my clothes are filthy from all the dust in the attic."

At the bottom of the steps, he stopped. His gaze swept over her, slowly, seductively and with great precision. His lips tilted into a wicked grin. "You forgot to mention the smudge on your cheek."

"Garrett, what's going on?"

He palmed her face, and with his thumb he wiped at the streak of dirt he'd found. "Come with me, cinnamon girl. Where I want to take you it won't matter what you're wearing."

From the glint in his eyes, she suspected he didn't want her wearing anything at all. That both scared and excited her. Every muscle in her body clenched in anticipation; every fiber sent welcoming vibrations for whatever he had in mind. Her brain, however, wanted to put on the brakes.

He looked around, picked up a notepad from the counter, jotted down a few words with a pencil, then tossed it on the kitchen table.

"What are you doing?" she asked cautiously.

"We might be a while. I don't want anybody to worry about you."

Be a while? Her eyes widened, and she swallowed hard.

"Look, Garrett, I don't think we ought to start anything at this late date. You'll be leaving for Orlando soon, and I—"

An instant later, she squealed like a stuck pig as he hefted her over his shoulder. She could scarcely be called petite, yet he carried her easily—right out the front door.

"Garrett..." she warned.

"Will you stop arguing, woman. I'm trying to do something romantic here."

"You call carting me around like a feed sack *romantic?*"

"I'm a real sentimental kind of guy. This will be something you'll be able to tell our grandchildren."

He put her in his sports car. Mute with shock, she sat very still as he snapped her seat belt in place. *Our* grandchildren? Donnie's children? Or was he talking about something more than that?

She was silent, and more than a little curious, as he drove them up into the foothills, taking the winding road with the speed and ease with which he did everything. Afternoon clouds had built over the distant peaks, and the setting sun streaked them with silver. The warm air blowing in the car windows caught her hair, teasing the loose strands across her cheek.

She was very nearly afraid to breathe. Certainly she couldn't manage a coherent thought.

He pulled into the entrance of the lake picnic area, but instead of parking he followed a narrow service road that traced the curve of the lake and led well away from where the crowds gathered.

Her heart stumbled.

She knew exactly where he was taking her. That secluded spot where they had first made love. When he came to a stop at an iron barrier across the road, she was still paralyzed with emotions churning in a combination of hope and fear and wanting all at once.

"End of the line," he announced, hopping out of the car. "Out you go."

Numbly she followed instructions. She found him

at the car's trunk, where he pulled out a wicker picnic basket and handed her a blanket.

"Would you please tell me what's going on?" she pleaded.

Giving her a cocky grin, he hooked his free arm around her waist. "Do you remember this place?"

"Of course I do." How could any woman forget the place where she'd given her heart—and her virginity—to a man like Garrett?

"I haven't been back here since that night," he said. "Without you, I figured it wouldn't be the same."

In the tiny sheltered cove, twilight had already settled across the sandy beach and filtered through the trees that hid the area from prying eyes. He set the picnic basket down, took the blanket from her and spread it on the ground. He sat and tugged her down beside him. A moment later, he'd produced candles, two wineglasses and a bottle of champagne. He popped the cork.

"Pretty romantic for a jock, huh?" He filled both glasses and passed one to her.

"Yes. But why all the trouble?" He probably could have seduced her right in the attic if he'd made the effort. She simply had no resistance to the man.

He touched his glass to hers. "To us, Charity. That's what this is all about."

She sipped warily. Her heart was a fragile organ. She wasn't sure how many times it could be broken and still be repaired.

He sat with one arm resting on his upraised knee. "Eight years ago, I should have trusted my instincts, Charity. I knew you were someone special. Someone, that if I had an ounce of sense in my head, I'd want to be with for the rest of my life. But I was young and stupid, and when you didn't return my phone calls it never occurred to me that I ought to get off my high horse and find out what was wrong. So, like Bud..." Looking sheepish, he shrugged. "I let it slide. It was the dumbest thing I've ever done. And it cost you so damn much."

"You don't have to blame yourself. Maybe if I hadn't been so unsure of myself, and so afraid I couldn't compete with all those cute cheerleader types that flocked around you, I would have made a bigger effort to locate you. And not taken your father up on his offer."

"Like you said, all that's in the past now." He took another sip of champagne. "I know I don't have much to recommend me as husband material...."

She drew a quick breath, her heart tumbling in a somersault, and her glass nearly slipped from her fingers.

"I've already botched one marriage, and I didn't even get as far as the altar. But I swear, if you'll marry me, I'll move heaven and earth to make you happy."

She waited for more, the words she had longed to hear and thought she never would.

"Do you love me, Garrett?" Or was she simply a consolation prize as she'd feared all these years?

"God, Charity. How can you ask? My gut's in a knot so tight, it's like I'm being strangled. If you don't say yes, I don't know what I'll do."

"Then say the words, Garrett. I want to hear you say you love me as much as I love you."

He took her face in his hands, and she felt his

fingers tremble like the leaves on an aspen tree. In the candlelight, she saw his struggle, his need and his love.

"I have never felt like this in my life. I love you, Charity Arden, more than I'll ever be able to say. But I'll show you every day if you'll let me. Please say that you'll marry me."

"Oh, yes, Garrett." Her heart soaring, she kissed him. "I love you so much. We'll move to Orlando right away and we'll—"

"Whoa! Wait a minute. What do you mean we'll move to Orlando?"

"You don't think I'd leave you in the clutches of all those beautiful groupies, do you? Besides, I've already decided to sell the farm. It's too much for me to handle alone, and Bud and Hailey want to move out. Now that we've got some equity in the place, I thought—"

"What about Rambo?"

She blinked. "Rambo?"

"You can't desert him. He's Donnie's pet. It would break the kid's heart."

"He'll adjust," she said, knowing it wouldn't be easy for either of them to think of Rambo turned into pork chops.

"I've got a better idea." He stretched out on the blanket, pulling her with him. "How would it sound to you being the wife of a novice pig farmer and the new Grazer High football coach?"

"Coach Riddler's quitting?"

"Retiring. He's asked me to step into his shoes. I thought I'd give it a try."

"But Orlando... Your career—"

"I've made a choice, sweetheart. Even if I could

be sure I'd end up with a Super Bowl ring—and nobody could guarantee that—I would rather stay here with you and Donnie. I've had my shot in the NFL. Now I want something more. The family I've been missing."

"Oh, Garrett…" she sighed, overwhelmed by the intensity of his love.

Cupping the back of her head, he brought her mouth to his. He kissed her with exquisite tenderness, nibbling on her lower lip, tasting her with his tongue. Though she could feel his tension, he took his time, arousing her with slow, measured strokes. It didn't matter where they lived. Only that he loved her and they were together. A family.

In the darkness, with only the faint glow of two candles, he undressed her. He loved her as though it were their first time together. And she loved him in return as though they had been partners forever, anticipating his needs, thrilling at his desire for her, giving every bit of herself and accepting all that he offered.

WHEN THEY RETURNED to the house, only a single light burned in the living room.

They slipped down the hallway to Donnie's room.

"Hey, sleepyhead," she said. She stroked his curly hair, inhaling his little-boy scent, and wondering if all their children would look like Donnie, or if she'd also be blessed by a child who resembled his father. "Can you wake up a minute?"

The boy rolled over and blinked. "Hi, Mom. I had strawberry-shortcake ice cream. It was real good."

"I'm glad, son."

Donnie's gaze flicked to Garrett. "It's too late for checkers tonight. Maybe tomorrow." He started to roll over.

Charity pulled him back. "Honey, I know you're sleepy, but this is important. We need to talk—just for a minute. It's about your father."

His eyes widened and he blinked. "Huh?"

"I've never told you who your father is because...well, it's hard to explain." She glanced up at Garrett in search of some help.

He sat down on the edge of the bed. "I'm your dad, son. I didn't know that till just recently but I'm so proud that you're mine, well, I'm pretty much popping my buttons."

Donnie frowned.

"See, the thing is, son," Garrett continued, "your mom and I are in love. I'd like to ask your permission to marry her so we can be a family."

"Would that mean I wouldn't have to have Homer for a dad?"

"Not ever, son," Garrett said. "You and your mom would be mine."

The boy blinked once. "Way cool." With that, Donnie turned over and was once again fast asleep.

Charity met Garrett's gaze and grinned. "At least you rate somewhere above Homer."

"Guess I have my work cut out for me, huh?"

"Not with me, you don't." Leaning forward, she kissed him. "I love you, Garrett Keeley."

"I love you, too, cinnamon girl."

Epilogue

It was the biggest wedding Grazer's Corners had seen all summer.

It was also the only one where the bride and groom had actually managed to exchange their vows without some disaster occurring.

Charity looked around the hall at the country club, amazed she, of all people, would be having her wedding reception here and that half the town would attend. But with Garrett and his father footing the bill, how could she object?

Bud and Hailey were there, of course. So was Donnie, though for the moment Charity had lost track of him. He'd been adorable standing up with Garrett as best man, solemnly presenting the ring right on cue.

In the corner, she spotted Kate Bingham, now Mrs. Mitch Connery, having landed the cowboy who'd stolen her right from the altar. Fortunately the former groom-to-be, Moose Harmon, didn't look all that miserable with the blond Betsy Muller on his arm. It looked like things might be heating up in the cosmetic department at Harmon's store.

From her spot at the head table, she cast her gaze around the room again.

Jordan Grazer was so in love, she glowed. She was looking up into the eyes of the man who used to be the town bad boy, Tanner Caldwell, a reformed rebel if Charity ever saw one. It also turned out he was a security expert worth megabucks, fully a match for Jordan's snooty parents.

Idly Charity wondered if she looked at Garrett with as much love and passion as she saw in the eyes of both Kate and Jordan for their men. She supposed she did. It would be impossible not to, the way she felt about Garrett.

To Charity's delight, Homer had accepted her invitation to the wedding and had come with a darling young woman on his arm, the romantic lead from the current production at the local little theater group. She wished them both the happiness she felt.

Returning from wherever his groomly duties had taken him, Garrett whispered in her ear. ''The photographer says it's time to throw the bouquet. You ready?''

She clasped the fragrant flowers, mostly wildflowers with a single rose in the center. ''I hate to part with it.''

''I'll buy you as many flowers as you want, sweetheart. But these you've got to toss to the next lucky girl. It's tradition.''

She remembered how she'd caught—inadvertently, she was sure—Jordan's bouquet as she'd been swept away by Tanner on his motorcycle. At the time, Charity had never expected she would be the next to marry.

But then, perhaps catching a wedding bouquet—

at least one in Grazer's Corners—had more powers of prediction than she had ever anticipated.

Garrett escorted her to the patio area the photographer from Modesto had designated for the shot. She'd checked out his credentials, and although she'd rather have been in two places at once, both as bride and photographer, she thought he'd do a credible job. She certainly hoped so.

The single women gathered around, though there weren't all that many. Charity prepared for the big toss.

"Mom! Watch out!" Donnie screamed. "Rambo followed us into town. He's on the loose!"

She whirled.

Rambo was lumbering through the country-club grounds, a man with a flailing golf club fast on his heels. Charity tried to dodge the onslaught of a thousand pounds of pork on the hoof. People screamed. Garrett, always quick, grabbed her around the waist, and in the process dislodged her bouquet, sending it into an arc over Charity's head.

At the last moment, Rambo veered away from the crowd. He and the golfer raced toward the eighteenth hole.

Behind her, Charity heard titters and shocked laughter.

She turned to find Agatha Flintstone clasping the bridal bouquet, her cheeks bright as a summer sunset, and her eyes glued to an equally mature gentleman they'd all come to know as Mr. B, a close friend of Jordan Grazer Caldwell's new husband.

"Interesting," Garrett commented, finally relaxing his grip on Charity's waist.

"Hmm, do you think Agatha's about ready to

give up her fantasies of Norman conquerors for something made of flesh and blood?''

''I don't know about her, cinnamon girl. I'd just like to get out of here as soon as possible. I figure our honeymoon is about eight years overdue.''

Charity agreed. And with Agatha still holding the wedding bouquet, Charity and Garrett slipped away. No one in Grazer's Corners was likely to miss them. By tomorrow morning, there'd be a new topic of speculation at the Good Eats Diner.

Smiling lovingly at her new husband, Charity decided she definitely preferred it that way.

Catch more great HARLEQUIN™ Movies

featured on the movie channel

Premiering September 12th

A Change of Place

Starring Rick Springfield and Stephanie Beacham. Based on the novel by bestselling author Tracy Sinclair

Don't miss next month's movie!
Premiering October 10th
Loving Evangeline
Based on the novel by *New York Times* bestselling author Linda Howard

If you are not currently a subscriber to The Movie Channel, simply call your local cable or satellite provider for more details. Call today, and don't miss out on the romance!

100% pure movies.
100% pure fun.

An Alliance Television Production

PHMBPA998

MEN at WORK

All work and no play?
Not these men!

July 1998

MACKENZIE'S LADY by Dallas Schulze

Undercover agent Mackenzie Donahue's lazy smile and deep blue eyes were his best weapons. But after rescuing—and kissing!—damsel in distress Holly Reynolds, how could he betray her by spying on her brother?

August 1998

MISS LIZ'S PASSION by Sherryl Woods

Todd Lewis could put up a building with ease, but quailed at the sight of a classroom! Still, Liz Gentry, his son's teacher, was no battle-ax, and soon Todd started planning some extracurricular activities of his own....

September 1998

A CLASSIC ENCOUNTER
by Emilie Richards

Doctor Chris Matthews was intelligent, sexy and *very* good with his hands—which made him all the more dangerous to single mom Lizette St. Hilaire. So how long could she resist Chris's special brand of TLC?

Available at your favorite retail outlet!

MEN AT WORK™

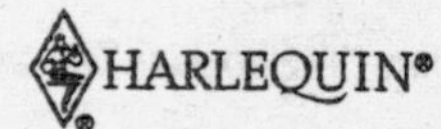

Look us up on-line at: http://www.romance.net PMAW2

Under an assumed name, a woman delivers twins at Oregon's Valley Memorial Hospital, only to disappear...leaving behind the cooing twin girls and a note listing their dad as D. K. McKeon. Only trouble is, there are three D. K. McKeons....

So the question is

WHO'S THE DADDY?

Muriel Jensen

brings you a delightfully funny trilogy of one mystery, two gurgling babies and three possible daddies!

Don't miss:

#737 DADDY BY DEFAULT
(August 1998)

#742 DADDY BY DESIGN
(September 1998)

#746 DADDY BY DESTINY
(October 1998)

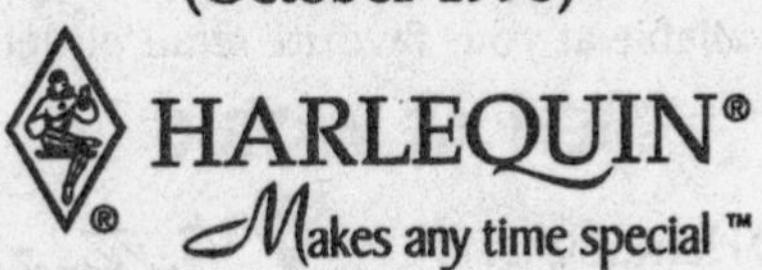

Look us up on-line at: http://www.romance.net HARWTD